The Drifter's Revenge

The job in the Montana timber camp for the railroad meant nothing to the drifter, Ryan. It was just another paycheck as he rambled west toward Oregon. But then he had seen the railroad company men gun down his friend Ben Comfrey over seventy-four dollars.

Ben had a widow and a son needing that money to get them through a hard winter and so Ryan took a hand. The railroad bosses first tried to laugh him off, then they tried to kill him. With fury in his heart and a capable gun in hand, Ryan now went after them instead.

He had set his mind on vengeance and was going to pursue it to the end of the line.

The Drifter's Revenge

Owen G. Irons

A Black Horse Western

ROBERT HALE · LONDON

© Owen G. Irons 2006
First published in Great Britain 2006

ISBN-10: 0-7090-7904-4
ISBN-13: 978-0-7090-7904-0

Robert Hale Limited
Clerkenwell House
Clerkenwell Green
London EC1R 0HT

Typeset by Derek Doyle & Associates, Shaw Heath.
Printed and bound in Great Britain by
Antony Rowe Limited, Wiltshire.

ONE

The near at hand cracking sound and the following barrage of falling debris were like a cannonade being loosed off overhead, and I dove for cover, rolling from the path of the felled eighty-foot pine tree. Ben Comfrey, experienced sawman though he was, had miscalculated and the massive tree, influenced by the gusting wind, had missed its mark by twenty feet or so; me, by much less than that. I lay on my back against the pine-needle-littered earth, covering my eyes with my forearm against the downfall of cones, bark and twigs as the big tree settled into the rising dust.

'Are you all right!' Ben was shouting. 'Ryan? Are you OK?'

I peered up at him through the branches of the fallen tree and grinned. 'Just. Thank God that's the last one. I've had enough of lumberjacking to last me a lifetime.'

Ben cleared away the smaller branches around me with a hatchet and dragged me to my feet to stand among the broken limbs of the white pine. I was shuddering a little. I blamed that on the cool wind sweeping up the pine-clad slope and not on the near miss of the tons of timber. Taking Ben's hand I stepped through the maze of branches and we crouched down in the clearing beside the bones of the huge tree. I wiped my forehead; Ben Comfrey lit his stubby pipe with trembling fingers.

'That was a near one, all right,' he said unnecessarily. I only nodded.

We had both come to Montana's Milk River country to spend a few weeks dropping timber for the railroad which was making its first forays into the northern plains. Myself, I was headed to Oregon, but then I had been headed in that direction for almost two years. Indians had slowed my passage, and the long winters. Maybe laziness.

I took my time wherever I traveled, liking the long sweep of the hills and the sudden upthrust of the massive bald mountains, the large game and small. I had to face it, I was a rover and if I ever did make Oregon, it was likely that I would get fiddle-footed within months and be back on the long trail to nowhere in particular.

'That's enough of that,' Ben said, echoing my thoughts. He was a square-faced, dirt farmer from over Billings way. He worked hard at his farming, but trying to come up with cash money in those times was enough to bring him out to the timber stands. Like me, he knew that winter was coming in fast in that north country and the idea of earning enough pocket money for beans, flour and salt to see us through winter was appealing.

The fall-crew was moving in now. Tough Irishmen, fresh over from the old country whose job it was to trim the boughs from the fallen tree. They didn't give us much more than a passing glance. We were amateurs who had no right even to be near an axe or two-man saw. If that pine tree had flattened me, they would have marked it up to my own inexperience and certainly shed no tears.

'They can have this job,' Ben said, finally getting his pipe lit. 'I'll shovel stables from here on if I have to.'

I had to agree with him. Not only was the work back-breaking, it was supremely hazardous. We had seen two men fall to their deaths from the trees – one of them from one hundred feet up while 'topping' it with a double-bitted axe. His leather strap broke and he cartwheeled through the sky to the ground. No one paid much attention. It was considered a hazard of the trade.

Another man, a boy really, had chopped off his own foot with one of the heavy, razor-edged axes and bled to death within minutes. My own advice to anyone who wants to go lumbering is to pause, get your head examined, and marry a shop-keeper's daughter.

Anyway, for us – Ben and me – we were done with lumberjacking. We started down the forested slope, Ben with the two-handled saw slung over his shoulder, and made our way toward the pay tent as the skies to the north began to gray and clot with clouds. We knew we had finished the job for the railroad none too soon. Winters in Montana are harsh and even the sap in the big trees freezes.

'I still don't see how they're going to finish that bridge before winter,' Ben said. We stood on a low granite outcropping looking out at the trestle the Colorado Northern Railroad was fixing to erect across the Yellow Tongue Gorge. Whitewater raced through the narrow canyon bottom, moving like the Furies. The beginnings of the trestle, clinging skeleton-like to the eastern rim of the gorge, lifted 150 feet into the cold skies. The gorge itself was 1,500 feet wide there. It would take a lot of time and skill and a lot of timber to reach the western bank.

'Myself, I don't care if or how they make it,' I answered. I was weary and cold and the birds over-head were telling me it was time to travel south before the blinding heavy snows of winter began. 'Let's collect our pay and ramble. Unless you want to stay on here?'

I won't tell you what he said in response. It was multi-syllabic and very harsh. The wind was up to near thirty miles an hour and the sky was closing, the temperature somewhere near forty when we checked the crosscut saw into the equipment shed. Considering, we saddled our horses in the stable, not wanting to hang around longer than necessary after we got paid, and trudged to the railroad office to take care of business.

It was a hastily thrown up affair of unpainted, mismatched lumber sitting in a tilted position on the side of the stump-strewn hillside. White smoke rose from its iron stovepipe, promising warmth. I started to feel better. The day hadn't yet gathered into snowclouds. The cold wind was moderate. My muscles and raw callused hands were no worse than they had been for the weeks of lumbering. Now with the prospect of hard cash in hand and a hotel room away from the vermin and man noises in the bunkhouse, spirits were lifting. I followed Ben Comfrey up the three steps to the shack, scraping my boots before we entered the close confines of the pay shack.

Behind the counter Jerrod Lucas sat, a thin, balding unhappy-looking man who handled the petty cash for the railroad. He looked sour, but then he always did. He must have been weaned on pickles. In one corner, tilted back on a wooden chair sat 'Sad Sam' Tremaine. Him, I did not like. The man had a cat-like grace, but his eyes were those of a fox. I don't know what his official title was – if he had one. His only skill seemed to be breaking up fights that erupted among the tired and bored lumbermen by breaking their skulls with the muzzle of his Colt .44.

As I say, he had only one skill. But he was very good at that.

I ignored his coal-black eyes as Ben and I went to Lucas's counter and presented our paybooks.

'You two leaving?' Lucas said, as if it were a surprise to him.

'Our agreement called for three hundred spar logs,' Ben replied, removing his hat. 'They're cut – there's the foreman's notations in our books. We've had enough of this work. We're drawing our pay.'

'Sorry you're leaving,' Lucas said, studying our paybooks through his thick spectacles. 'But I guess with winter coming on. . . .'

'That's it,' Ben said. 'I can still bring in my winter wheat and with a little spare money, the wife, kids and I will make do until spring.'

'The only problem . . .' Lucas said, straightening his glasses with a forefinger, 'is that the boss is not here to authorize this.'

I was dimly aware of the elevated legs of the chair 'Sad Sam' was sitting in, coming down to the floor.

'Yeah, we know that,' Ben persisted. Mr Alton McCallister, manager of the Colorado Northern crew had departed for New Madrid on the line train a week previous. The weather, he said, was not good for his arthritis. 'What does that have to do with us? We done our work; we want our pay.'

I could see a little fire building in Ben's eyes, so I touched his arm, crossed my forearms on the puncheon counter and tipped back my hat. I tried smiling. 'We just want our wages, Jerrod.' I turned my small blue paybook around again to look at my figures. 'Seventy-four dollars and fifty cents for me. Ben must have about the same due him.' I nodded at the company safe in the corner. 'I know you've got that much poked away somewhere.'

'The boss would have to sign it off,' Lucas said. 'I told you. He's not here.'

I was vaguely aware of Sam Tremaine's bootsteps shuffling across the wooden floor behind me. Ben, he was furious.

'You damned crooks!' he exploded. 'My family is waiting for me to get home with that pay.'

I tried remaining calm although I was as unhappy as Ben. 'See here, Jerrod, we fulfilled our side of the bargain. Two months felling at thirty-five per, plus extra pay for the two Sundays we worked. I know seventy-four fifty isn't a lot to you, it isn't a lot to a big company like Colorado Northern, but it is to us. How about you just fork over our wages and we'll leave.'

'I need Mr McCallister's signature to disperse any monies,' Lucas said, and this time he said his piece with a little sideways smirk. Probably because he knew Sad Sam was right behind us. 'The only thing you could do now would be to ride to New Madrid and find Mr McCallister. Show him your paybooks and have him write me a note.'

'That's a hundred miles down and a hundred back!' Ben shouted. 'God knows when the blizzards are going to hit.'

'It's company policy,' Lucas said, and then his eyes lifted and he side-stepped away. I knew what was coming. I threw my elbow back wildly and ducked. When I came up from my crouch I saw that my elbow had gotten Sad Sam in the wind and he was sort of bent forward, his jaw a welcome target for my clenched fist. I'm not the biggest man in the world, but the hard life of work I have led had toughened my muscles. I got Sam with a solid blow and he staggered backward, dropping his Colt before he came up against the plank wall and sort of slid down to sit on the floor.

11

Ben hadn't moved, but Lucas had, surprising both of us as he cut loose with a shotgun. Aimed straight up, it created a new smoke vent in the roof of the flimsy ceiling. I grabbed Ben by the arm and we raced toward the door of the shack. Very early on I had learned not to argue with a twelve-gauge scattergun, right or wrong.

We broke through the leather-hinged door; at the same time. Sad Sam, having recovered his wits, snatched up his revolver and leveled two or three shots at us, tearing great splinters from the wall of the shack. Nearly simultaneously we saw a group of Colorado Northern workers emerge in a confused crowd from the timber. I don't know what they thought the shots were about – Indians, robbers, murder – but here they came streaming down the muddy slopes waving axes and pistols. Ben and I raced for the stable and jumped onto our ponies' backs.

I spurred my black horse's flanks, startling it, and he leaped into motion. Ben, on his stubby roan was just yards behind me. There were some wild following shots fired. I don't think anyone knew what he was shooting at, but a group of men with guns in their hands kinda feel obliged to cut loose with some lead on general principles.

I was racing the black horse down through the pine and cedar-clotted hillside toward the dark flats below when I saw Ben just tilt to one side and then the other and fall from the saddle, rolling twice to the cold earth where he lay still while his roan stepped on its reins, tossed its head in confusion and finally came to a ginger-stepped walk. I didn't know what had happened to the roan. It seemed to have lamed itself. I was concerned only with Ben Comfrey.

I spun my white-stockinged black around and rode that way, dismounting on the run. When I reached Ben and crouched down, I could see the blood leaking from his mouth.

'Bastard shot me,' Ben said. He was having difficulty with his words. I don't know who it was that shot him. Maybe Sad Sam Tremaine, maybe one of those wildly firing lumberjacks.

It didn't matter. Ben was a goner.

I knew this from the color of the pink blood and from the froth in it. He had been lung shot and there is no bandage or doctor who can stop that sort of bleeding. I lifted my eyes to the hillrise where blue spruce and lodgepole pine crowded the skyline to assure myself that no one was now pursuing us. Then I sighed most heavily, sat against the half-frozen dark earth and put Ben's head on my lap.

'It's nothing, Ben. Only a nick. I'll get you into New Madrid. I hear they've got a real Eastern doctor there now.'

'That so? Have they got a real preacher?' Ben said, and he closed his eyes. A few minutes later he did say, 'Ryan – my wife needs that money.'

Then he didn't say a thing more. Just out of reach of his hand I saw his stubby pipe. The bowl was stained with blood. I closed his eyes. The roan had come near with seeming misery in its eyes. It

13

nudged Ben with its muzzle, but, of course, the dead man did not respond.

I rose, dusted the mud and dampness from my Levi's and waited a long minute, deciding. Then I swung into the black horse's saddle and headed south. Maybe, if the weather held, I could reach New Madrid within the week and hold a conversation with Mr Alton McCallister, the manager of the construction gang for the railroad. I didn't know. I just knew that somewhere near Billings, Ben Comfrey's wife was waiting for her man to come home, bring in the winter wheat and provide for the long coming months with the hard money he had earned.

Maybe it wasn't my job, my duty, but, as I said, I hadn't been headed anywhere in particular to begin with. Besides, I could use that $74.50 too. As they say, it's not the money, but the principle. Well, this was both. I still found myself feeling guilty about Ben's body, but there hadn't been time to dig a grave with all those railroad people after me, and carrying him day after day on the trail was impractical. I had gathered up Ben's paybook, the scuffed wallet he carried, his Colt and gunbelt and jammed them into my saddle-bags.

His roan had followed along for a while, not knowing where else to go. But I had checked him over briefly and felt the heat in its foreleg and knew it had strained or torn a tendon there. I had stripped off Ben's saddle and bridle and set the roan loose. It followed us for a few miles, limping pathetically, and then gave up hope of keeping up with the black and just disappeared into the wilds.

Then, with the cold wind following I had started south toward New Madrid, down along the Wyoming line. There was a man there I needed to talk to.

TWO

My luck wasn't holding at all. By nightfall the snow had begun. Not the heavy blanketing fall of mid-winter, but what was being driven down from the tangled sky by a rising wind was just as cold. Along about five o'clock I could no longer see where I was riding. I rode the black horse up into some thicker timber and eased my way along the trail until I found an upthrust of granite that cut most of the northern wind. You couldn't call it a shelter of any kind, but I figured I could survive well enough on the lee side until morning. I wrapped my blankets tight around me and, with my horse tethered, leaned back to watch the dark trees dancing and bowing, yielding to the bluff winter. Even the largest pines swayed before the driving wind. It was frozen hell, enough even to make me long for that ratty, stinking barracks back along Yellow Tongue.

I pulled my hat as low as it would go, hunched my shoulders as high as they would go and crossed my arms, thrusting my gloved hands into my armpits. It didn't do a lot of good as far as warmth was concerned, but maybe it was for the best that I couldn't even catch forty winks.

Because they came at me in the hour before midnight. Three men, one mounted, two afoot, leading their horses. The mounted man was Sad Sam Tremaine – I knew him by his yellow and red mackinaw even in that light. And by silver cloud-filtered starlight I saw the glint of a blue-steel revolver in his hand. I shoved myself to one side and shot before I was ready. It was before Sam was ready as well, for I saw him stand in his stirrups and then throw out his arms. Of the two men afoot one drew his Colt and fired wildly and the other took to his heels, running while he tried to mount his horse at the same time. The man who shot at me I had tagged in the chest with the .44.

I don't know to this day who he was, only that he had come to hunt me down and kill me. The fleeing man I let go as I stood and listened to his horse's hoofs pounding away and fading into the distance.

I approached the two men I had shot. Sad Sam made a few muffled, inhuman sounds and that was all as I reached him. The other gunman was only a silent dark form against the new bluish white of the snow.

I didn't know who might be behind on my trail so I saddled the black once more – something he did not appreciate, gathered the reins to the other horses and worked my way southward through the thin snow.

17

An hour or so later an eerie half moon, silver and small, appeared playing tag among the remnants of the clouds. I swung down and crunched around in the snow, making a more manageable tether for the two horses I was leading with a length of my riata, something no former cowhand ever rides without. For a while, as I tied my slip knots on to their bridles and checked them for snugness, I had time to think. What I wondered was why they had come after me at all. Over $74.50! That seemed crazy. All I could think of was that maybe Sad Sam, Lucas, maybe some of the other were making some extra money by cheating the casual laborers. It didn't seem that a big man like Alton McCallister could be bothered with such small-scale thievery. They said that McCallister wasn't a millionaire, but he was close enough so that it didn't matter.

Maybe that was how he had gotten so wealthy, though. You never knew. I thought I would ask him that question one of these days soon.

I swung back into the cold saddle, shivering all over and headed on, watching the eastern sky steadily, wishing for the sun to rise. When it did finally loom above the hills to the east, red and low and flattened, I knew why so many of those ancient peoples had worshipped it. Hour by hour it grew warmer and I was able to strip off my long coat and tie it on behind even though the cold wind was constant and the skies continued to cast promises of gloom across the snow-mantled plains grass.

The creeks, when I forded them, were fringed

with ice. The morning sun caused the long-grass plains to shed their snow, but early nightfall froze the land to an ice-sheathed, moon-shadowed wilderness again. I kept my pace steady. Now and then I would shift horses. The gray – the one Sad Sam had been riding – was obstinate and liable to treacherous moves. Like his owner, I mused. The lithe sorrel the other killer had used was smoother, but given to timidness when it couldn't find the trail.

I would set them free soon, I decided. It was too much trouble leading them. I would let the Indians have them. That was the winter the plains were so empty of them, however, that I found myself almost wishing that they were back. The Nez Perce had all gone north to Canada to try escaping the wars; the other tribes – Cheyenne and Sioux – had followed their ancient pattern and drifted south to follow the buffalo with the onset of winter. Of course, there weren't that many bison left even this far north, but the pattern was long-established and if they couldn't find the big herds, they were at least travelling with the sun. For the time being I continued on with my small remuda.

By the third day I had reconsidered a few matters. After being attacked I had wanted to lose myself in the vastness of the empty land. Now, as my trail cut across the eastern leg of the Colorado Northern Railroad's right of way, I wondered if I might not be better served following the tracks straight into New Madrid. It was a shorter, surer route, and there was the chance I would run across a way station along the line where a man could get some hot food ... and that was what finally convinced me. My growling stomach had gotten spoiled with that timber-camp fare, three meals a day and plenty extra if it was wanted.

I started to follow the silver rails, straining my eyes into the distances, looking for some desolate depot where the locomotives could bring water and firewood aboard to fuel the great steam engines as they made their clanking rush westward.

It was nearly sunset again – cold, harsh and blowing – when I had my first bit of luck.

With the shadows long and crooked beneath my horses, I just picked out a faded streamer of smoke rising against the ragged skies. Paralleling the new-laid railroad tracks, the source of the smoke drew out of the shadows, proving to be a hastily built depot. The station house itself was low, strongly built of two-inch thick planks with only narrow slit windows cut into the wood. (Someone did not believe that the Indians were gone from the plains for good.) The water tank was green-painted steel mounted atop a framework of wood, its spout raised cobra-like to await the needs of the locomotives which would one day arrive. On the opposite side of the tracks was a newly built stable, the wood still clean from the distant sawmill. It wouldn't take long for the north country winter to weather it to splintered gray. Near it, but far enough away to distance it from the stable smells, was what I decided must be a planned hotel and perhaps restaurant. Right now it was only a half-framed skeleton with a pile of new lumber sitting in a damp pile beside it.

I held my course for the depot structure where smoke rose to be whipped away in the gusting winds. It promised shelter and warmth and the probability of food. All that I could have wished for just then. I swung down and looped the reins of the black to the green wood hitchrail, glanced at the other ponies and then to the darkening sky where the sun dropped leadenly toward the Rockies in the far distance, appearing deep orange and suffering.

I scraped off my boots and went in the open door.

A narrow man with a pleasant smile and a full set of gray whiskers looked up at me, unsurprised, from the puncheon table where he had seated himself.

'Saw you coming a mile out,' he said amiably. 'I sent Paco back to start some coffee.'

'That's kind of you,' I said, as the man gestured me to a seat opposite his at the table.

'It's the least we can do. You're the first man we've seen in three days. Paco and I get along all right,' he lowered his voice, 'but he don't speak very good English.'

At that moment the man, Paco, emerged from a smaller space at the back of the depot, separated from the main room only by an Indian blanket that been hung as a divider. Paco was unsmiling, small, quick in his movements, and dark. I took

21

him for an Indian, but he could have been Mexican. He placed tin cups of coffee in front of us and glanced at me quickly, his eyes barely meeting mine.

'Put the man's horses up in the stable, will you, Paco?' my host said.

'Yes, Mr Tagg,' Paco answered. He looked at me again from the corner of his eye and then went outside, closing the door, leaving us in an amiable half-darkness. The coffee steamed. A lantern glowed dully on the wall above a counter of undressed lumber. There was nothing in the room by way of decoration, nothing to indicate its function.

'I am, you might say, in on the ground floor,' the bearded man said, noticing my inspection. 'They practically built this place around me.'

'Your name is Tagg?' I asked, removing my hat to place it on the table.

'Taggart. Paco doesn't like to use more syllables than he's forced to.' He smiled and sipped at his coffee. I could hear the horses being led across the railroad tracks to the stable, their hoofs sounding against the crushed rock laid between the ties.

'Lonesome out here,' I commented, 'and going to get more lonesome when the big snows fall.'

'You are right there ... pardon me, what did you say your name was, son?'

'Ryan.' He waited expectantly, but that was all I provided. Usually a man in the West didn't give out his full name unless he felt comfortable doing so, or unless it was demanded. Neither case applied

22

here. Taggart shrugged.

'You're right that it's lonesome here,' he said, tugging at his beard with his fingers before he sipped again at his coffee. 'In earlier days, Ryan, I spent five months snowed in by myself in the high-up mountains. Beaver trapping I was. Somebody had convinced me that it was a way to get rich easy and quick when all those dandified people were mad for beaver top hats. Lonesome – now *that* was lonesome. And those Colorado mountain snows make Montana look like paradise. Drifts twenty feet high in front of the door of my shack . . . anyway, I have seen lonesome. It don't bother me. Besides, I don't have wife nor family; I'm too old to have a girlfriend back somewhere to moon over.'

Paco had come back in, a gust of cold devil wind following him through the door. He approached the table, said something I didn't catch and wasn't meant to hear to Taggart, and tromped off into the kitchen again.

'He asked would you like a beef steak and some beans. I reckoned you would, so I sent him back to heat something up.'

'I appreciate it,' I said, drinking some of the rapidly cooling coffee.

Taggart leaned back in his chair, interlacing his gnarled fingers across his narrow waist. 'So, Ryan, what was it you found to work at out West? I know you're not a trapper and I didn't see any prospecting gear.'

The question could have been intrusive, but it seemed the old man was just in need of some conversation, so I told him. 'I was lumberjacking. When the snow started I decided it was time to collect my pay and head out.'

'Wise of you,' Taggart nodded. I noticed that Paco had emerged from behind the Indian blanket again, but he wasn't carrying a tray. His hands were behind him. Taggart's face seemed to draw slowly together, to tighten and grow hard.

'You should have cut those horses loose, Ryan!' he shouted suddenly, and I saw his hand drop toward his holstered belt gun. 'They're wearing railroad brands.'

I moved forward, not back. I hefted the heavy puncheon table toward Taggart and ducked low as Paco pulled a pistol from behind his back and began firing wildly. The table edge had pinned Taggart's legs to the floor and he howled with pain. I could see his hand scrabbling at his holster and I kicked it with my bootheel, hearing bone crack.

Taggart howled again and I drew my own Colt, peering up over the upended table. Paco was dancing sideways along the wall with his smoking revolver in his hand. There was unmistakable fear in his eyes, and if he had taken to his heels, I would have let him escape through the front door, but he turned, crouched and fired at me again. My bullet was a little quicker. It caught him in the throat and Paco pitched forward into a puddle of his own blood.

Taggart was cursing, keening and groaning all at once. I yanked his pistol from his holster and stood over him, panting. I glanced at Paco, but he did not move so much as an eyelid.

I looked down at Taggart's fear-contorted face, cursed myself for my bad luck and picked up my hat.

'Don't shoot me,' Taggart begged.

'I'm not going to shoot you, you damned fool,' I said angrily. 'If you had let me talk, I could have explained it all to you. I'm no horse-thief and I'm no killer.' Then I again shifted my eyes to Paco's still form and told him. 'It looks like it really is going to be a lonely winter for you now.'

I left him to his personal misery, collecting the two rifles and the revolvers I found scattered about the station. Then I stepped out into the gusting wind and blowing light snow, stamping my way to the stable.

I found the kerosene lamp hung on a nail inside the door and lit it. I threw the weapons I was carrying up into the hayloft, startling the horses that were stationed there, each in his dry stall. Paco had paused to give all of them a forkful of dry hay, apparently, for the gray and the sorrel after my brief interruption lowered their heads again to nibble at their fodder. Two other horses were there, looking at me with no apparent interest.

My own white-stockinged black, on the other hand lifted mistrustful eyes toward me as I entered. He knew what sort of perfidy I was capable of. Here he had just found a warm haven, had his saddle stripped and been given good dry hay and I had returned to demand who-knew-what of him. I set about brushing him down while he returned to his meal, checking hoofs and legs for soundness, because the animal's instincts were right. We were going to be back on the trail sooner rather than later.

I had no way of knowing if Taggart had another hidden weapon I had not found, or if other riders might be approaching – either from the timber camp or from New Madrid. I gave the black a bucket of water and when he had drunk about half as much as he wanted, I placed his saddle blanket on his back, smoothing it. He gave me another evil look and then stood there resignedly allowing me to finish my business.

With the bit slipped in and my saddle cinched, I led the horse to the double doors at the front of the stable, blew out the wick of the smoking lantern and moved cautiously out into the cold, devil dark night.

The first hundred yards I covered quickly. Then I turned up my collar, patted the resigned black's neck and continued on my way to New Madrid to have a few words with Mr Alton McCallister of the Colorado Northern Railroad company.

THREE

I didn't freeze or starve before reaching New Madrid, but it seemed that both possibilities were near along the way.

New Madrid wasn't much of a town, but it was bigger than any I'd seen for a time. The first thing that caught the eye was the gleaming locomotive with two attached Pullman cars sitting at rest before the two-story, gingerbread-decorated depot. They had painted the new building white with green trim. A balcony ran along the face of the upper story. Nobody was there, of course, since the trains had not yet started to run and would not until spring arrived and the Yellow Tongue Gorge trestle was finished, but just seeing the spanking new building must have brought some civic pride to the heart of the community. In those times having a railroad stop in your town meant that the outpost was destined to survive the tenuous life on the plains. Many a town after a hopeful beginning died quickly and mercilessly as the railroad bypassed it.

Main street was nothing special. Facing rows of low wooden buildings looking at each other across a muddy, snow-flecked and rutted road. At intervals there would be a false front rising to give the impression of a second story. There were four or five buildings with an actual second floor, and a low brick building that looked very stodgy. There was no sign on its blank face. A bank, I thought, or possibly a jail. Now and then there was an attenuated side street where planks were laid for people to cross without sinking into the mud. I passed something like two dozen wagons – Conestogas and freight rigs, parked every which way, and five times that many horses. There weren't a lot of human citizens out in front of the buildings on this icy day.

They had clustered in the restaurants – I counted four – and in the saloons. I saw at least a dozen of these. One of them had a tinkly piano playing inside. Once I saw a large woman wearing something of shiny yellow showing all of her legs and most of her top, beckoning to me from an upstairs window. She looked wearier than I felt. I waved at her in passing.

As the weary black and I plodded along the muddy road, I reflected there was still no way that anyone could call New Madrid a beautiful mecca. It was miles short of a place like Denver where – I had been told – the silver and gold magnates had built opera houses and had indoor bathtubs with gold plated faucets. Still, it was far from the way I remembered it. In those times there had been nothing but a few squat sod houses and mournful cattle tramping through fields of withered corn.

The railroad, I could see by the number of new buildings, had brought in a conviction that was bursting to grow and blossom into a queen of the plains. It was the railroad, then, that held primacy. And it figured that the man I wanted to talk to would be New Madrid's most honored resident. It wouldn't do to stride up to Mr Alton McCallister in full public view, take him by the collar and demand my $74.50; I'd likely find myself jailed or lynched. Mr McCallister was a very substantial man and I was a wilderness tramp.

For the moment I put the consideration of how to contact him aside and decided to take care of first things first. I had one silver dollar and a stomach cramped with hunger. I swung down in front of the first restaurant I saw, tied up the black and went inside. The warmth was a glory. There were two waitresses bustling this way and that with trays of food and steam rising from the kitchen beyond the seating area, which was furnished with round wooden tables and stiff-backed wooden chairs.

The smell of food was overpoweringly tempting, the warmth a cozy blanket across my cold shoulders, the hard wooden chair a joy to my saddle-sprung legs. I removed my hat, rumpled my straggling hair and sat peacefully waiting to give my order. No one paid any attention to me. I guessed that almost everyone in was a recent arrival and they hoped for and expected more in the boom to come with spring when the trains would begin to run west.

People came and went, ninety per cent of them men, ninety per cent of them rough-looking and wild. New Madrid hadn't been a town long enough to develop any sort of gentry.

I let my stomach know it hadn't died on the vine. Ham and beans, apple pie and half a cabbage soaked in rich butter. I hardly glanced up. There was nothing more interesting to me at that moment after three days on the trail than what rested on the huge platter before me.

I did notice one man in brown trousers and white shirt wearing a dark coat over in the corner. He had a gray walrus mustache and seemed interested in me for some reason. Tilted back with his chair leaning against the wall, he studied me with weary eyes as I ate.

My first consideration was that he might have been a lawman – he had that substantial, somewhat sad look about him – but there was no telegraph wire yet running from the lumber camp or the railroad depot where the trouble had taken place, and so I dismissed the idea that he was looking for me. The thing was – as I have pointed out – that almost everyone in was a stranger to everyone else, so me being a new arrival couldn't have attracted his attention that much either.

I shrugged it off mentally, paid my bill, received a few coins in change and pocketed them. I replaced my hat and walked across the plank floor into the bright, cold day. My black horse looked accusingly at me as if it knew more trouble was afoot. I surprised it by untying it from the rail and walking it up the muddy street to a shambly stable.

'We're closed!' someone hollered, before I had even gotten into the shade of the horse-smelling structure. In seconds, a wide-shouldered, big-bellied man appeared, trying to button up a too-tight twill jacket. 'No more business today. I got to lock up.'

The man's round face was red with excitement. His pouched eyes were a little wild.

'Hold on a minute,' I said. 'Is there trouble?'

'Trouble? My wife's delivering, mister. I got to get home and Isaac, my stablehand, didn't show up!'

'Want me to watch the place for you?'

He looked at me as if I were a godsend. 'How much?' he asked cautiously.

'Just free lodging for my horse. And, if you think it's fair, some hay for me to sleep on tonight.'

He didn't hesitate. He had crammed a greasy hat on his head and briefly shook my hand. 'Done! Just watch the place until I get back. I can't miss the baby's coming, but I can't afford to shut down either. Isaac – I'll strangle him!'

He was halfway to the door before he turned to say across his shoulder, 'No whiskey, no smoking!' And then he was gone and I was left alone in the shadows of the stable. It was warmer in there than it was outside. The horses gave off a deal of heat and the plank walls cut the cold north wind.

Smiling to myself, I decided that *everything* can't always go wrong. I unsaddled the black, slipped its bit and rubbed it down as it fed on new hay and a bucket of oats I had borrowed – figuring that as part of the hasty deal I had made with the stable-keeper.

I raked some hay into an empty corner stall and lay down, my stomach full, the cold wind absent. No one was shooting at me and I was as comfortable as a man can be. It doesn't take a lot to become comfortable when things have been so rugged.

I rose only three times that morning. Two men with a mule team pulled up and we unhitched their animals and led them inside. One tall young cowboy came to claim a long-legged bay horse, muttering that he didn't care what they said – Texas winters were the tropics compared to Montana and he was riding south before the true blizzards visited. One old bird with a little whiskey in his belly came in and wandered around the stalls a bit, examining the horses.

'Damn me!' he said. 'I don't know where I could have lost old Paint,' and he wandered away.

I was through with my napping by then. I lit the lanterns, for it was growing toward dusk outside and there was a streak of crimson in the long sky. I made myself useful by raking up a bit, then resorting to the shovel and wheelbarrow. About the time I was finished with that, the stableman returned.

His shirt was unbuttoned, his face had gotten florid from alcohol or excitement or both. He was smoking a fat cigar. He clasped me as if I were his oldest friend in the world.

'It's a boy!' he yelled, throwing his head back.

'I'm naming him Bartholomew.'

'Congratulations,' I said.

'Bartholomew Givens! You like that name?'

'It's fine, Mr Givens. I'm sure he'll be a joy to you and the wife.'

'That's right, he'll be . . .' He was out of breath and sagged to sit on a nearby hay bale. He kept his cigar clenched between his teeth. 'Do I know you?' he asked.

'Ryan,' I told him. 'I know it's been a crazy day for you. I've been watching the stable for you. You told me I could park my horse and myself here for the night.'

'That's right . . . that's right.' He rubbed his broad face. 'Like you say, I've been a little over-excited today.'

'A man has a right,' I told him. 'Is this your first child?'

'First one, yes, first one. Frightening in a way; it all worked out fine. The wife's well; perky. I'll have to try it again some time,' he mused.

I left him to his thoughts although he obviously wanted someone to talk to on this night. Well, I still had someone I needed to talk to – Alton McCallister by name, the railroad's line manager. I tucked my shirt in, buttoned the sleeves and went out into the bitter night to try finding him.

There was the matter of $74.50 to be settled.

During the day I had taken the time to go through Ben Comfrey's scant belongings, hoping to find an address where I could send his money to his widow. Of course, if she didn't live right in town

33

in Billings, there wouldn't be one, and Ben said he had a little two-by-four farm on the outskirts. The thing was, I didn't even know her name. You see, in those days, preachers and all were spread awful thin across the untamed West. Not a lot of these parsons were skilled Indian fighters and they weren't all that eager to venture into the wilds. It could be that Comfrey's marriage wasn't even of the legal sort. It had been known to happen.

In Ben's pack I came across a German silver-framed daguerreotype of a woman and a small flaxen-haired boy. Their sepia faces looked out at me intently. They were standing on the porch of a cramped-looking sod house A lonesome elm tree drooped on one side of the building.

The kid looked serious and maybe a little older around the eyes than was right for his age. The woman, to my surprise, appeared to be no more than eighteen or nineteen. Therefore, she could not have been the boy's mother – of course, I could have been wrong; guessing ages is difficult. She was very small, her eyes wide and trusting but nearly fearful. Her hair seemed to be dark brown, coiled on the sides of her head like some Swiss girl. Could that young thing be Ben Comfrey's wife? No matter – all that mattered was getting his money to the folks it belonged to. I hadn't even considered composing a letter. I didn't want to write one that began 'Your husband was murdered. . . .'

I had put all of those thoughts aside as I went out on to the dark Montana street. First things first. I would get my money and Ben's from the railroad.

I had just emerged from the stable when I noticed the man in the shadows of the restaurant's awning across the street smoking a fat dark cigar, eyes pondering me. Enough light shone through the windows behind him for me to recognize him and his silver walrus mustache as the person who had been watching me earlier in the restaurant. He made no move; I gave him no notice, but I felt rather than saw his hooded eyes following me as I walked up the street, the rime crunching underfoot as the day's muddy slush froze.

I was thinking only of Alton McCallister. I had never met the man, and I had seen him but once up on the Yellow Tongue. Prosperous-looking with red hair so thin you could see through it to his bare scalp. He was narrow and tall. He wore a gold watch chain that swayed across his stomach. He had a tie tack that must have held a diamond the size of a pea. His clothes were tailor-cut and his narrow reddish-brown mustache was tightly clipped. Beyond that I knew nothing of the man's habits, methods or inclinations.

McCallister might have been a thief, a good-natured grandfather, a womanizer, a cut throat – anything at all. All I knew of him was that he was wealthy and that wherever he had ensconced himself, it was going to be in luxurious surroundings.

New Madrid, Montana, was not rife with luxurious accommodations. There were, as I've said, a dozen or so saloons all roaring on this evening as I walked the frozen streets, but I didn't expect to find him in one of these gin joints throwing away his money on the spin of a wheel or the flip of a card. Wealthy men don't grow wealthier by gambling, and to me it always had been evident that the wealthy always have a need to grow still wealthier.

The finest hotel in town, as far as I could see, was a two-story white-painted monstrosity called The Palace. Gingerbread dripped from every eave and four wooden columns supported an over-hanging portico. Surreys arrived and women in long dresses and tiny hats were handed down to step to the boardwalk in front of the hotel.

I stood watching for a minute, scraped my boots and straightened my trail-duty clothing as well as possible and started that way, crossing the muddy street.

The man with mustache was behind me, moving slowly, heavily from shadow to shadow.

The entranceway of The Palace blazed with light from the chandeliers behind. I approached the heavy double doors and a man in some sort of silk-livery with the face of a Welsh miner sidestepped in front of me, blocking my way.

'Are you a resident here?' he asked in a gravelly voice.

'Not yet. I was hoping to find a room,' I replied.

'You ought to try the Tumbleweed, bub. They got rooms there for two bits.'

'Maybe I have more than two bits, partner.'

'Then you can get two rooms,' the unbending doorman said.

'Look, pal,' I said, 'the truth is, I need to find Alton McCallister. I thought he might be staying here.'

The big-chested man looked across my shoulder and spoke to me out of the side of his mouth. 'You're looking in the wrong place, friend. Try the railroad cars.'

I nodded my thanks. 'I appreciate it,' I told him.

'Yeah, well, beat it now, would you? I got a job to hold on to.'

I don't know how the encounter would have worked out if I had known McCallister was in there, but I imagined it wouldn't have been good for my cause. The doorman, bouncer – whatever he was – had given me the tip I needed, however; I made my way back across town under the light of a cloud-fringed silver moon toward the depot, the standing locomotive and two Pullman cars.

I didn't figure I would be any more welcome there than I had been at New Madrid's swankiest hotel, but that didn't matter. I was going to have my talk with McCallister and that was that. The night wind snuck through the alleys and twisted bits of paper down the street. The occasional leaf-less tree cast odd moon shadows against the rime-coated mud. Uptown the piano banged at intervals and then had its sound torn away by the rising winter wind.

The monolith of the train sat just beyond the last building in sight. A stray dog looked at me, snarled and then slunk away, its tail curled under. I made my way toward the railroad cars. The car directly behind the diamond-stacked 4-4-2 loco-motive was dark. Apparently anyone inside that Pullman was asleep beneath warm coverlets. Soft music played from inside the second car where lights blazed and kerosene lanterns burned hotly. I could smell cigar smoke and beneath that the scents of bay rum and talcum powder. I made my way to the rear of the car.

A guard in a buffalo coat rested there on a wooden chair. He had his boots propped up and a Winchester rifle cradled in his arms. He was drowsy and slack, but when he saw me he came alert and he came quickly to his feet.

'Who's out there?' he demanded. 'What do you want?'

'Take it easy, brother,' I said, lifting my hands. It does no good to argue with a Winchester in the dark. 'They sent me down to report to Mr McCallister.'

'*Who* sent you?' the guard asked suspiciously, as the muzzle of his rifle lowered.

'I'm down from Yellow Tongue timber camp. There's problems out there.'

'What kind of problems?'

'If I explained it to you, you still wouldn't under-stand. I've got to talk to Mr McCallister. It's company business, friend.'

He looked at me uncertainly, glanced at the interior of the lighted Pullman car, shrugged and answered, 'I've got to see if it's OK.'

'I understand. Make it quick, would you,' I said, dancing a little. 'A man could freeze out here on a night like this.'

The guard vanished into the interior of the car, a brief cloud of smoke and sound emerging as he did so. I looked up to the stars for a moment, wondering just how crazy I really was. After a few minutes the man with the rifle reappeared. He carried the Winchester loosely in his hand now, however, and he waved me up the iron steps.

'The boss says to come on in,' he told me and, after I took a brief glance back at the big-shouldered mustached man who was watching me from the depot shadows, I clambered up the steps and followed my watchdog into the interior of the opulent Pullman.

FOUR

It was like stepping into another world, entering that railroad car. That's exactly what it was, of course. These gentlemen in their stiff shirts and their ladies lounging on red velvet settees with their satins and lace had no idea of what life was outside of their warm cocoon, out where the cold winds blew.

I had to unbutton my coat quickly or faint. The interior of the car had to be at least seventy degrees. There were two free-standing wood-burning stoves, one at each end of the car, both black iron embellished with yards of brass filigree. Six or seven men, well-shaved and barbered, sat around an octagonal card table with green baize covering. Stacks of poker chips and sheaves of bills sat in front of them. They were smoking long cigars and laughing, sipping from crystal glasses. A woman's dark eyes peered up at me over the black lace of her fan. I turned to my escort.

'McCallister is the one seated next to her,' he told me.

Then I vaguely recognized the red-haired, mustached man with the prominent thin nose. He had cutting pale-blue eyes that followed my progress as I approached. The card players looked up at me in passing with various degrees of interest or disdain. I halted before McCallister. He rose slowly to his feet.

'Tom says you're down from Yellow Tongue,' McCallister said in a baritone voice. He had his coat open, his thumbs in his trouser pocket. He watched me curiously, with a sort of impatient prodding in his eyes.

'That's right,' I said quietly. People were listening, and I didn't want them to catch what I had to say; there was no point in provoking their interest.

'What is it, then?' McCallister said loudly, unconcerned with what anyone else might hear. 'Trouble with the trestle?'

'Not that I know of,' I answered. 'Could we step aside into some more private place?'

'Not necessary,' he snapped. 'What is it that you want to report?'

'It's a matter of pay, Mr McCallister.' I pulled the two worn paybooks – mine and Ben Comfrey's – from my coat pocket and explained. 'The railroad owes me seventy-four dollars fifty as you can see.' I offered him the paybooks but he declined to accept them. 'And the same amount is due to my friend Ben Comfrey. I have his book because he was killed along the trail. I need the money; Ben's widow will be needing it.'

I didn't expect him to laugh, but he did. Long

41

and loud, throwing his head back as he looked around at the other well-groomed influential men in the car. 'You've come all this way for seventy-four dollars!'

'And fifty cents. The same for Ben Comfrey.'

He never heard the end of that sentence. He had begun laughing again. A woman smiled and turned her head away; a man at the poker table chuckled and slapped his hand on his thigh.

'This isn't meant to be funny, Mr McCallister,' I told him, feeling a coldness begin to trickle down my spine. Maybe it was easy for these men to laugh over a month's pay. It wasn't that easy for me. I wouldn't be eating, my horse wouldn't be fed if I didn't collect. Ben Comfrey's wife would be up against a hard Montana winter without supplies.

'Go on back and talk to the paymaster,' McCallister said, moving his hand dismissively.

'I already have,' I said, feeling my face flush a little. 'He wouldn't cough it up.'

'Why not?' the railroad boss asked with a crooked smile. 'Is it because you didn't earn the money after all? Maybe you just found these paybooks,' he said, slapping at them with the back of his hand.

'No, sir. He wouldn't pay us because someone is a chiseler. Someone is cheating the trusting hard-working men you hired.'

His smile was gone in an instant, hardened to a tight scowl. 'Are you saying that I am a welcher – that I would resort to such petty machinations?'

'I haven't figured that part out yet, McCallister,'

I told him. 'Maybe it was the paymaster; maybe it's you; maybe it's the whole railroad. All I know is that I want my pay. That's why I came. Give it to me and I'll be on my way and you can get back to your poker and your whiskey and your lady friends.'

Maybe I had gone too far. This man wouldn't like his pride being chipped at among his friends. Nevertheless, I was right. Now I had had my say. He could have scooped up ten times what he owed me from the corner of the poker table and given it to me. He didn't.

He made a gesture like a man dusting away an insect and motioned toward the front of the car. Another rough-looking man I hadn't seen before started making his way toward us while the one called Tom stood behind me with his Winchester.

'Escort this man down the line,' McCallister said. He stepped away and I clutched at his coat sleeve.

'Listen . . .' I said, and then from the corner of my eye I saw Tom raising the stock of his rifle. It crashed against my head sending off thundering bells inside my skull. Before I could hit the floor the other man had caught me under the arms, and together he and Tom dragged me to the back of the Pullman and out into the frigid night. My head was swimming and my heart seemed momentarily to have stopped beating. I could feel hot blood trickling down my scalp. I tried to fight my abductors off, but my arms and legs were moving like those of a four-year-old child's, like a man trying to fight his way out of a dream.

The wind was in full icy rage. The door to the Pullman slammed behind us, cutting off all warmth and sound. On the platform, I heard Tom ask, 'Well, what do we do with him?'

'McCallister said to take him down the line. I don't think that meant just dump him to the side of the road here.'

'No, I guess not,' Tom said. He hit me in the face for good luck. 'Damn you! I don't want to be out in weather like this.'

But we went, the three of us. Tom's friend arrived with a buckboard and they threw me into the back of it. We bounced away behind two steaming horses flying down a rutted road into the dark distances. The wind remained firm and cold. My teeth chattered and I drew up into a fetal position, trying for warmth I couldn't find.

It seemed we drove on for hours. My face gathered jagged splinters from the weathered bed of the old wagon. The blood had quit leaking from my skull, but my head still throbbed on unbearably. I must have passed out at least once, because I don't remember the wagon being drawn up beside the trail, only rough hands being placed on my legs and shoulders and being thrown out on to the frozen ground.

The buckboard turned and started away. There was not a light to be seen on the vast prairie from horizon to horizon. I tried to rise but couldn't. I closed my eyes and prepared for the worst. In the darkest hour before dawn it began to snow again.

I rose stiffly like a man's shade emerging from a

frozen grave. Rising, the full blast of the snow and wind hit me full in the face. It was numbing; if there had been a place of shelter I would have curled up there for as long as it took the storm to pass. There was no such place. Blinking into the sting of the driven snow, I started walking. There was virtually no visibility, but I knew that wind was driving out of the north, and so I kept my face into it using the wind as a primal compass, bowed my head and slogged on over broken ground. If I didn't find the railroad tracks soon then I would turn to my left, knowing I had been dumped to the north of the tracks, but I thought it had been to the south of them.

Not that I had much memory of the events. I was moderately surprised that I had survived the night. It seemed Tom and his partner were not stone cold killers at least. I tugged my coat more tightly around me, trying to fight off the waves of icy wind. Snow had collected on my shoulders and head. Touching my skull, I winced with the pain. It was not bleeding, but my hair was matted in a saucer-sized scab at the back of my head. I kept my eyes turned down, straggling on. My hat had been lost of course, but they had carelessly left my pistol in its holster. I would have more use for that Colt than for the hat before this was over.

I tripped over an unseen rock and fell down. That set off the flaring pain in my skull once more. I rose and walked on blindly. Once, during a brief clearing of the day, I thought I saw a small building off to the south, but it was far distant and my hopeful eyes might have been playing tricks on me. I needed to find those railroad tracks, otherwise I was going to walk right past New Madrid and continue wandering on the lonesome plains until I was frozen and exhausted. Then I would simply lie down never to rise again, not to be discovered until spring when the weeds would grow tangled through my bones.

Two fleet shadows slunk past me and I grabbed for my Colt. Even through the curtain of the blown snow I knew that they were skulking prairie wolves. I braced myself, but they went on. Apparently they, at least, knew of some secret den in which to shelter up as the storm passed.

I didn't have their instinct. I plunged onward, falling once, then again over rocks and roots hidden beneath the inches of fresh snow. Once the clouds parted and an amazingly brilliant shaft of sunlight touched my eyes with blinding illumination. The clouds closed again and the snow continued. I fell again. My heart was pounding; my eyes burned. I knew I had the strength to rise, but it didn't seem worth the effort.

Then I saw what I had tripped over. My fingers reached out and touched frozen steel. I had found the railroad tracks.

The knowledge energized me. I struggled to my feet and turned to my left. My head was still bowed, my legs heavy, but I moved with refreshed purpose. The town was ahead. McCallister was ahead.

I was going to live to see them both again.

With the weather as it was I couldn't be sure of

the passing hours, but I believed I had reached New Madrid just at dusk. I staggered from the railroad tracks and moved into the first alley I saw. The wind was cut by the buildings standing there. It no longer worked the snow like miniature sabers against my eyes. I felt warmer, safer. I could have sat down in that alley and slept. There was a much better place for that, if sleep could come to me.

I worked my way out on to the main street and started on wobbly legs along a boardwalk. There was no one else on the streets, although I could hear sound from behind the lighted windows of the saloons. Some of the men had apparently decided to ride out the storm inside these boisterous shelters.

I stepped from the boardwalk, staggered, and crossed the frozen street. No one had come that way for a long while – the snow was undisturbed against the dark earth except where my boots cut fresh tracks.

Smelling it before I saw it, I gave a silent cry of relief. The stable was just ahead of me. I walked toward it, exhaustion weighing heavily on me now. A lantern burned low as I entered. The horses stood looking at me curiously, my white-stockinged black among them, wondering no doubt where his mentally unhinged master had been wandering now. I made it all the way to my pile of straw before I collapsed and slept for years in the warmth of the horse-smelling building. I could hear the wind outside, but it had no meaning to me now. I was a man in shelter, a man alive.

'*Hey*!'

I felt a boot toe nudge me, but I was too exhausted to rise. I tried opening an eye, but that seemed to demand too much of my precious energy. The boot toe nudged me again, not so gently this time.

'Hey, you! Ryan!'

I opened one eye and rolled over, coming out of the depths of the dark cavern I had been sleeping in.

'What are you doing back here?' the voice asked. I recognized it and managed to sit halfway up, bracing myself on my elbows.

'Hello, Mr Givens,' I mumbled.

'What are you doing back here?' he asked. He stood there holding a kerosene lantern with the wick turned down low, the smoky light casting concerned shadows across his face. 'I told you that you could stay here last night, but you never came back. Left your horse. What'd you do, get drunk?'

'No, sir. I got myself beat up.'

'Oh?' Concern flickered briefly through his eyes, but vanished. 'I told you that you could sleep here last night, didn't I? For helping me out while my wife was birthing?' I nodded and he went on, 'That don't mean you can live here with your horse eating free hay. Isaac saw you here and it troubled him. You've got to be moving on.'

'All right,' I muttered, sitting all the way up. My head hung for a minute before, looking around, I braced myself against the planks of the stall and rose. Givens grew apologetic.

'I mean I know it's hard weather out there and all, Ryan, but I can't just let every saddle tramp and hard luck cowboy bed down here. This is a business, you know?'

'I know. I'm sorry,' I said. 'I'll be moving on. Can I wait for dawn?'

'It is dawn, Ryan. Still dark outside, but the storm's blown over and there'll be a bright new sun in an hour or so. Just right for riding on your way.'

I didn't say anything. I could not argue with Givens's logic, and he had done me a favor. 'Did you notice if the train is still in the station?' I asked.

He took a moment to follow that leap in my thoughts, but answered, 'Far as I know it is. Where else would it go?'

'Just wondered. Thanks.' I patted my pockets and was surprised to find I still had enough silver change for breakfast. As I came fully awake and the sky outside began to glow with a soft orange color, that idea seemed more compelling. Givens turned off the lantern and watched quietly as I saddled my black horse and gave him his bit.

'You weren't lying about getting beat up, were you?' he said.

'No.'

'You ought to see the back of your head. Your jaw isn't all that pretty either. Plus you got some bad splinters in your cheek.' Then, grudgingly, he suggested, 'Why don't you draw yourself a bucket of water from one of the barrels and rinse up? I think I got an almost clean towel in the office.'

I ground-hitched my horse and drew a bucket of water from one of his six oaken barrels. Kept inside, of course – you can't get a horse to eat ice when it's thirsty. When he came back he brought me a newly stropped razor, a sliver of yellow lye soap and a comb with a few missing teeth. He showed me where he had propped up a plate-sized bit of broken mirror and left me to my task.

I appreciated what he had done. When you have nothing and a man helps out, you don't forget. I've seen it before, many times. Take one of those dudes at the Palace Hotel out for champagne and oysters – or whatever they eat and drink – and he'll cut you the next time he sees you if your fortunes have changed. Give a truly hungry man a sandwich and he'll remember it a long time.

I eased the long gray splinters I could find from my cheek and chin, seeing, as Givens had told me, that when Tom had slugged me for ruining his pleasant evening of guard duty, his fist had swollen my face and it was starting to color nicely to purple and green.

Then I soaped my face and shaved gingerly. My natural face emerged slowly from behind the thicket. I soaked my head good and then began the most painful operation of all – trying to comb the huge scab from my scalp without tearing open the gash underneath again.

I finished the best I could, parting my hair and combing most of it to one side. Peering into the mirror, I saw my own features, only slightly puffed and discolored and decided I didn't look any worse than half the men in town after a night out. I wished again that I had my hat. It was a pearl-gray Stetson that I'd given fifteen dollars for long ago in Great Falls. There's nothing like a good Stetson to warm your head and top off a well-dressed man (which I wasn't at the moment). And there's nothing like wandering around bareheaded in Montana in the wintertime to make you stick out among the crowd.

'Well, that's a change,' Givens said, as I handed back the gear he had loaned me.

'I appreciate it,' I said with feeling. I rubbed my smooth jawline and grinned. 'Say hello to the wife and little Bartholomew for me.'

Then I took up the reins to my always wary black horse and walked him across the slushy road toward the restaurant I had eaten at before. The sun was rising like a huge molten sphere. The slush underfoot would be a foot of mud before high noon. People were emerging from their nesting places, rubbing their eyes, looking east as if they had never seen a winter sun before.

I hitched up the black and tramped into the restaurant, leaving muddy bootprints behind me like everyone else.

Breakfast was tinned peaches, four hotcakes and three eggs followed by a quart of coffee. I was beginning to feel almost alive. My momentary serenity was crushed as I paid my bill and realized that now I was as close to stone broke as a man could get and the only way to get any funds was to brace down the railroad thugs and grab Alton

McCallister and force him to choke it up. It wasn't a pleasant prospect.

I stepped out on to the boardwalk with a tooth-pick between my lips and got myself arrested.

A snake-quick hand slipped to my holster from behind and removed my Colt. Another hand had taken my left wrist and pulled my arm far up my back. A voice asked me softly, 'Can we do this gently, or do we need to make a spectacle of ourselves.'

I glanced at the people milling on the board-walk in front of the store, their eyes fixed on me, and I said, 'No need to make a fuss. I'd lose anyway, it seems.'

My arm was released and I turned to see the big man with the walrus mustache and the sad pouched eyes holding my pistol loosely. My first instincts about him being the law had been right. I could just see the tips of the starred badge he wore poking out from behind the edge of his coat. He smiled at me in a regretful way and started me off down the street while the populace watched.

We trudged through the mud toward the low featureless brick building I had seen earlier. Now I could see a small sign under the eaves that read 'Town marshal's office. City jail.'

We pushed on through the heavy door to the inside. The three small boys who had been follow-ing us along expectantly hoping for a ruckus walked away in disappointment.

'Coombs is my name,' the marshal said. He placed his hat carefully on his scarred desk, emptied my revolver of its .44 cartridges and placed it beside it, pocketing the bullets.

'Hey, Coombs, I see you've captured another desperate criminal!'

The voice came from one of two iron-barred cells deeper in the building. I could see a man there with his hands gripping cold iron.

'Shut up, Lennox,' the marshal said, shrugging out of his heavy coat. Coombs looked at a hand-written piece of paper on his desk and then back to me.

'I suppose you know why you're here?'

'No.'

'No?' Coombs scratched his head. 'I've got charges brought against you for vagrancy and for making menacing threats.'

'I don't know what that means,' I said honestly.

'Alton McCallister of the Colorado Northern says that you burst into his private Pullman car and threatened him with violence if he didn't give you money.'

'That's ridiculous.'

The sad eyes lifted slowly from the paper. 'He's got six witnesses.'

'I see.'

'How are we going to deal with this?' the marshal asked. 'Have you any money at all?'

'No.'

'All right. You admit the vagrancy charge.'

'I suppose, but I don't understand that law. I mean every place I've ever traveled they have laws against vagrancy,' I told him, feeling heat begin to flush my face. 'They just never explain how a vagrant is supposed to be able to pay a fine for vagrancy!'

'In my jurisdiction we work it off,' the marshal told me calmly. 'And then we send you on down the road to make trouble in the next town. That's not so serious – this business about threatening McCallister is.'

'Threatening? I asked him for my pay, that's all.'

'That's not what he says.'

'He's lying.'

'All the witnesses are lying?' the marshal asked, lifting one bushy eyebrow.

'Are they all employed by him?' I asked, expecting no answer. 'Look, I was invited into his railroad car. I told him what I wanted. He had two men beat me and dump me out on the prairie.'

'They say you started the fight and then ran off.'

'Do they?' I said. 'Doesn't the law say something about me having the right to confront my accuser?'

'I believe it does,' the marshal said. His eyes were quiet and completely inexpressive. 'However, Alton McCallister and his people have pulled out and returned to the end of the line – Yellow Tongue, that is to say – to check on the trestle construction. He won't be back for at least ten days.'

'Marshal?' I asked. 'How long does a man serve for simple vagrancy in this town?'

'Ten days or pay ten dollars,' he said without hesitation.

'I see.'

'It's banditry!' the voice from the cell hollered again. 'Simple legal banditry.'

'Shut up, Lennox!' the marshal said, the first time I had heard him speak with emotion. 'Now that you're sober, you think you're a lawyer?'

'I'd be one of the few that was,' the man named Lennox shouted back, and then he began to chuckle.

'You're going to have to do the ten days on vagrancy anyway,' Coombs told me, 'even if McCallister doesn't press the other charges.' He looked at my battered face a little doubtfully, dropped the paper back on his desk and seemed about ready to say something like 'sorry', but never did.

I was led back to the second cell, placed in it and watched as the marshal locked the door with a big iron key.

The other prisoner, Lennox, stood clinging to the bars of his cell, staring at me across the narrow aisle between us.

'McCallister, huh?' he asked, as I sank on to my bunk which was two planks hung from the brick walls from iron chains. 'Did you really try to hurt him?'

'No, but I almost wish I had,' I said, stretching out on the rough bunk.

'I wish you'd have broken his neck,' Lennox said. I peered at him, seeing a man with a round face and small boy's upturned nose sprinkled with freckles across a pasty hangover pallor. There was venom in his words.

'You have something against him?' I asked, sitting up.

'Yes, I do! The railroad right-of-way cut across my grazing land. It wouldn't have cost them nothing – nothing to them – to route their rails half a mile south. Now I have to fence off that end of the boundary. And in wintertime! That ground is froze solid. I fence it or risk losing cattle every time that iron horse rumbles through my land. Yes, I have something against him and the whole rotten railroad.'

'Have you tried talking to them. Going at them legally?'

'I'm not a wealthy man. You think I could go against a battery of lawyers like those the Colorado Northern has? No . . .' He seemed briefly miserable. 'Mostly I get drunk, spout off and end up in here for my troubles.'

He sagged on to his own bunk disconsolately. Well, I thought, at least I wasn't alone in my dislike of the railroad. We spent a silent half-hour in the dark cool cells side by side before Lennox sat up suddenly, grabbing at his head as if that movement had been a mistake. When he had recovered he asked, 'Look here, what name do you go by?'

'Ryan.'

'Tell me, Ryan, can you do ranch work? I mean, how are you with fencing?' he asked me.

'About average,' I answered.

'Average is all I need. Listen, I can use some help on the ranch. As I told you, I got to get some fencing done. That, and I like the way you stood up to McCallister. How about if I go your bail and get you out of here? Would you work for me?'

'I'm only hanging around here waiting for McCallister to get back,' I said in a lower voice.

'Ten days?'

'That's what the marshal said.'

'If you'll agree to a dollar a day for your wages, you'll have your fine settled with me by then. Besides, I guarantee you that working for me will be better than anything the town wants you to do to pay off that fine – and I won't lock you up at night,' he said with a smile.

I thought it over and couldn't find any reason not to take up his proposal. I nodded to him. 'OK, Lennox. After ten days, though, I'll be leaving you. I still am going to look up Mr McCallister.'

'Ryan,' he said, 'I might just go along with you when you pay him that visit. Whatever he owes you, he owes me more. Much more.'

FIVE

So it happened that after Marshal Coombs had decided that Art Lennox was sober enough to be no longer a menace to society, Lennox paid his own fine and ten dollars for mine as well. The marshal didn't seem to like it a bit, but he himself had set my fine and there wasn't much he could do about it. As for the other charges, he had also admitted that McCallister had left town without filing any official complaint concerning them, assuming I would still be in custody for the next ten days at least.

Coombs handed me my unloaded gun and the cartridges he had taken from it and walked us both to the door of the jail, watching as we walked up the street to where my horse still stood in front of the restaurant. We recovered Art Lennox's lanky little roan pony from the stable. A scarecrow of a man, that I took to be the unreliable Isaac, led the horse out, and we rode slowly out of town.

Lennox had been talkative back in the jailhouse, but now he was mute. I figured a hangover had smothered his high spirits. In less than an hour we were sitting on a low snow-dusted bluff looking down at Lennox's ranch.

There wasn't a lot to it, but it was nicely laid out and he was probably proud of it. His eyes glowed with satisfaction as we drew up and looked down at the low log house, an outbuilding which was probably a bunkhouse in roundup season, a small corral with two horses, tiny at this distance and, near a stand of leafless cottonwoods, twenty or thirty cattle. A creek wound its way across the land, its bottom clotted with dry willow trees. I could hear the hushed passing of the water as it flowed over boulders and among ice floes.

'Nice place,' I said for something to say.

'It suits me. I put a lot of labor into this spread. If you look south you can just see the sun on the rails. That's where we're going to have to start fencing. The east border we don't have to worry about – that's where the creek runs. We'll have to bring the fence line this way to abut the bluffs here.

'I hate like hell to fence land,' Lennox said gloomily. 'It shouldn't have to be fenced. And not because of some damned railroad cutting across my property.' His tone changed. 'The wife's at home,' he said, pointing a stubby finger toward the house where a faint curlicue of smoke could be seen rising from the chimney of the log house. He sighed. 'I guess we'd better go down and see how much trouble I'm in this time.'

We started our ponies down the snowy bluff.

The sky continued to hold clear and it might even have been a few degrees warmer. If the storm held off for another few days, I thought, we should be able to get the fencing done, especially if the frozen earth began to thaw.

We rode at a walk into the yard where patches of untrammeled snow remained. Beneath a huge oak tree Lennox halted his roan and told me, 'You go on over to the bunkhouse. Old Billy should be around somewhere; he'll fix you up.' He sighed heavily and added, 'Me, I've got to go in and catch hell from the wife – I don't want anyone to watch that.'

I nodded and turned my black horse toward the bunkhouse. I thought I saw the front door of the house open a few inches, but nothing was said as Art Lennox swung down, tilted his hat back and started up heavily into the porch.

The horses in the corral lifted incurious heads to watch as I rode past and tied the black to the hitching rail. I walked to the bunkhouse door, listened, and heard nothing. Unsummoned, I pulled the latchstring and let myself into the vacant, musty interior of the building, saddle-bags across my shoulder.

As my eyes adjusted, I saw a stove in the corner with a big black iron kettle and a big blue enamel coffee pot on it. There were three roughly constructed bunk beds with tick mattresses and leather webbing for support. Six men, I figured would be even more than Art Lennox needed at the busiest of times, but then, like all small ranchers, he must have had hopes of growing. There was a puncheon table with a deck of cards on it and three chairs scattered around.

'We got beef stew. It's still warm, or should be,' a squeaky voice said. 'If you want it hot, you build up the fire.'

The voice, I saw, came from what I had taken to be a roll of spare blankets resting on one of the bunks. Now the man stretched narrow arms and rose, walking toward me, peering at my face, his hands on his hips.

'You ain't Jarvis.'

'No.'

'Jarvis usually brings the boss home.' The man I took to be Old Billy walked to the pot and stirred it with a wooden spoon, tasting it. 'It's still warm, like I said. If you don't like beef stew, that's too bad. That's what I made. And I'm the one who has to carve the meat and tote the onions and potatoes, the carrots up from the root cellar. I get no help.'

'Beef stew sounds just fine,' I said.

'It better, it's all we got,' the garrulous old man said. He hobbled to one of the wooden chairs and seated himself carefully as if he might break. His shoulders were hunched and his hands gnarled. I guessed he had arthritis and this cold weather couldn't be helping any.

'What happened to Jarvis?' he demanded.

'I don't know him. I'm new here.'

'Jarvis always stops to play cards with me. And old Jarvis, he knows how to soften up Art's old lady so she don't tear into him. She says she's going to cut his ears off one day, and she just might do it!'

'What's their trouble?' I asked. I had found a tin plate and was spooning some of the thick stew on to it.

'Trouble!' The old man laughed without humor. I could see into the toothless hollow of his mouth. 'You seen it, didn't you? Art, he glums around here swearing and complaining about all the work he's got to do to keep the place together – then, instead of doing it, he rides off to town and starts sucking on a whiskey bottle.'

'I could see that a woman wouldn't like it much,' I said. I had found a spoon and, wiping it off on my shirt-tail, I proceeded to eat. Billy watched me with narrowed eyes, waiting for me to make a remark about his cooking, perhaps, but I had no complaints to make. It was just good honest beef stew in dark gravy, and since there didn't seem to be a shortage, I ate my share and then some.

After I had eaten and gotten my horse settled out at the corral to make new friends, I started out with Art Lennox toward the fence line sitting on the bench seat of his wagon. In the bed of the wagon were two spools of barbed wire and fifty or so split cedar posts. I wore a torn hat Billy had dug up from the collection of gear left behind by transient cowhands, rabbit skin-lined black leather gloves and my long leather coat.

Art didn't say much at all. His wife must have given his ears a good burning. He was morose, silent and probably still somewhat hung over. Now and then he would mutter something that I took to be addressed to the absent Mrs Lennox, but I paid no attention. There's no easier way for a man to get himself in trouble than by butting into domestic squabbles.

I needed no more trouble than I already had.

'I would have brought Billy with you, but he'd probably just slow you down,' Art apologized.

'I'll make do,' I answered. He glanced at me from the corner of his eye as the two horses pulling the wagon dipped down into a shallow wash and drew us up to the other side. There I could see the twin silver rails of the railroad running along a low rise.

'Did they pay you for the right of way?' I asked Art.

'They weren't required to,' he said bitterly. 'The state declared imminent domain. All for the public good, you know. Damn, I've still got twenty acres on the far side of the rails I can't even use for anything.'

Then he fell silent and, as he halted the wagon, he showed me what I was to do. There was about 150 yards of fencing to be thrown up here parallel to the tracks. The cedar posts had to be set at thirty foot intervals, cross-braced at the corners with the ends of the wire wrapped around boulders to anchor them. I could do it all right. I had fenced before, but as I told him and had to admit, I was only average at the work.

'Can you manage it in ten days?' Lennox asked, studying the layout. His arms were akimbo, the wind shifting his thinning dark hair. He had removed his hat to mop his brow after the briefest of exertions. He and I had unloaded a dozen or so posts and a spool of wire. The remainder would remain aboard the wagon, making it easier to move later on. The unhitched horses stood twitching their tails, tugging at the frozen yellow grass.

'On my own?' I asked with some surprise.

'I've got the rest of the ranch to run,' he said unhappily. I wondered why he didn't have at least one sturdy handyman around to help with things, but I said only, 'I'll give it my best, Art.'

'That's all I can ask. I got to have it done before the trains start running. They'd kill any roaming steer.'

'I understand that,' I answered. 'What about this man Jarvis to help if I start to fall behind?' The ground was still frozen down a way and the fencing itself wouldn't take half the time of the digging.

'Jarvis don't work worth a damn,' Lennox said, and there was no reply I could make to that.

'I do, Art,' I promised. 'You'll get your ten dollars' worth from me – now, then, if you'll let me have that digging bar?'

He sort of half-smiled and nodded gratefully. I walked to the creekline and began the first post-hole as Lennox, walking, led the team of horses back toward his ranch house where now a pretty plume of smoke rose from the chimney, promising warmth and the comforts of home. I hoped he could make it up with his wife and enjoy her comfort and the fruits of his own years of labor.

I worked on through the morning, opening the frozen ground with the bite of my digging bar. From time to time, I stopped to unbend my back and look skyward. To the north all was holding clear. There was a pair of eagles winging high against the azure dome of the sky and a raven who had taken an interest in me sat on a snowy hummock and croaked at me from time to time, tilting his head from side to side. I paused and looked up the railroad line, wondering if they were close to getting that Yellow Tongue Gorge trestle finished, or if the weather had held them back.

Wondering how long it would be before Alton McCallister arrived back in town on his private railroad car.

I thought to myself that a normal man would just have taken off and headed toward Oregon again, forgetting the railroad baron and that $74.50 I was owed. But now and then I could also recall how Ben Comfrey and I had talked at night and what he had said about his wife and kid and his tiny farm, loving them and hoping for a good future. I could see the faces of the young woman and the boy looking out at me from that stained sepia picture and thought of them waiting at home for Father to return. I thought of McCallister drinking his champagne and of his fancy women and I knew that I would stick it out to the bitter end.

The raven flapped his wings without taking to the air and gave a mocking croak.

Well, maybe the bird was right. Maybe I was

some kind of fool.

The sun began to float westward and not long after four o'clock the long shadows stretched out and began to merge and pool. Darkness would settle in soon. Art Lennox hadn't returned to check up on me, nor to bring a lunch. I straightened up, peering toward the ranch house, but I saw no sign of horses coming toward me.

The day had gone well enough. I had put down fourteen posts, tamped the ground firmly around them. The work had passed quickly. Now I was starting to grow cold, the perspiration beneath my coat chilling as I quit my exertions. The raven had left after an hour or so, growing tired of watching this inexplicable man-labor. I had seen a young mule deer along the creek earlier, but when it lifted its eyes and caught sight of me, it had bounded away. So it had been a lonesome but not unpleasant day. Now with the sky coloring and the temperature beginning to fall, it was time for it to end.

I placed my digging bar atop the cedar logs and started walking back toward the ranch. I hated leaving tools out in the weather; my father had drummed it into the heads of all of us boys that wood warps and splinters and those splinters are going to end up in your own hands. Iron rusts quickly, as well, but I didn't care for the idea of toting the bar back over my shoulder. With a touch of irritation I decided that if Art couldn't be bothered to bring me lunch or provide a ride back, I didn't much care if his tools rusted.

By the time I reached the ranch, the stars were out in cold silvery progression across a black, black sky. There was a light in the bunkhouse window and one in the main house. I was trudging past Art's yard, wondering if I should pay him a visit when the door opened a crack and then widened and a woman wearing a lime-green robe, her hair pinned up, stepped out on to the porch.

Art's wife was younger than I would have thought, her hair reddish-brown in the backglow of light from the fireplace within. She clutched the robe to her breast and raised a hand to me. I stopped and turned in that direction without going toward her.

She didn't say a word. Just stood there looking at me. I couldn't read her eyes in the shadows, so I don't know what message they might have been concealing.

'Is Art in there?' I asked. I still hadn't figured out if I was going to tell him off or not, but I did want to make a couple of points clear.

'No,' the woman said hesitantly. 'No, he isn't.' Then she backed into the house, still clutching her robe in front. The door closed silently and I was left staring at the dark house.

Shrugging, I stamped to the bunkhouse where Old Billy sat playing solitaire. He glanced up from his card game to tell me, 'Stew's on. It's good and hot tonight.'

I winged my hat toward my bunk and filled my plate. I sat down opposite Billy and asked him, 'Have you seen Art?'

'He went to town.'

'Supplies?'

'His own kind,' Billy said, placing a red eight on a black nine.

'Good God,' I exclaimed. 'You don't mean to tell me that he goes into town to drink whiskey every night!'

Billy raised rheumy eyes and shrugged his thin shoulders. 'Sometimes only three nights a week. It depends on how long his money holds out.'

'It's a wonder he has any.'

'It doesn't cost much to get drunk. It costs a lot to *stay* drunk,' Billy said cryptically. I had the feeling he meant more than he was saying, but it didn't matter to me. I had a plate of warm food and a bunk to sleep on. What did it matter to me what Art Lennox did to waste his life away? I had put in a day's work. I could endure nine more of them while I paid off my debt and waited for McCallister's return.

I had just finished that thought and the plate of stew, when I heard a knock on the bunkhouse door. It was a fluttering little knock like a bird beating its wings against it. Old Billy got up to answer it as I swiveled around in my chair curiously.

The door opened to reveal Mrs Lennox standing there, her face impatient yet somehow meek. She had changed her robe for a dark dress with red velvet collar and cuffs. Her reddish hair was pinned up and there was a touch of rouge on her cheeks. The dying sun to the west showed her off to remarkable advantage. Her voice was little breathless.

'Oh, Billy,' I heard her say, 'the fireplace in the house is smoking badly. I think something in the chimney has caught fire. There could be an owl's nest up there, or maybe it's just build-up, because it hasn't been swept for nearly a year. . . .' Her words rushed forth, a woman frightened. Old Billy just stood nodding, his shoulders bent. The woman went on, 'With this weather coming in, I have to have a fire. And if the house goes up!'

'I wouldn't know what to do about it,' Billy told her and she looked my way.

'Of course Art's gone when I need him. Henry Jarvis usually does these things, but he must be off trying to bring Art home again,' she said, with a long-suffering sigh.

She looked at me more intently now and asked, 'You're the new man, aren't you? Ryan? Could you please at least take a look at it?'

'I'd be happy to,' I answered, and she gave me a brief grateful smile and disappeared into the night. Old Billy was watching me as I put my hat back on and buttoned up my coat.

'That's a good-looking horse you got,' he commented laconically. I didn't get his meaning. He added, 'It's a quiet night, you could ride a long way on a horse like that.'

'I could,' I agreed, my eyes narrowing at the old man's words. 'But I owe Art Lennox some work, and I need to stay around. What's going on here, Billy?'

'I don't know,' he grumped. 'You'd have to ask Jarvis, I suppose.'

I shrugged at the enigma as he returned to his cards, and stepped out into the clear cold night to trudge toward the main house. Looking up, I saw no unusual burn or sparks issuing from the chimney, but maybe by now, if it had been something ordinary, like a big bird's nest, or more likely a little pitch flare, it had cleared itself out. Maybe the woman was simply uneasy with her husband away, afraid of fire – I couldn't blame her for that. I would at least take a look and try to reassure her.

She let me into the lighted front room. The firelight danced through her hair. She was a fine-looking woman, I thought, probably feeling alone out on the prairie and neglected by her husband. I took off my hat and crossed the plank floor to the fireplace, noticing the heavy Spanish-style furniture and the Indian blanket hung on the wall.

'Mrs Lennox . . .'

'You can call me Veronica,' she said. 'If you're going to work here, we should be friends.' She went on, 'Usually Jarvis takes care of these things.' Then she said in a halting yet husky voice, '. . . when Art's away, I mean.'

'The fire's pretty hot still,' I told her, crouching down in front of the hearth. 'There's no way of telling if it needs cleaning. From what I could see outside, the chimney's clear and there's no smoke in here.' Nor did I smell any. What I could smell now was the scent of jasmine soap and another, deeper indefinable scent as the lady bent over my shoulder to peer into the low-burning logs. I rose and turned toward her.

70

'Don't go,' she said, putting a hand on my shoulder. It was a nice hand, smooth with tapered fingers. There was firelight in her eyes now and I shook my head.

'I can't do anything about your problem, Mrs Lennox. You better wait until the cool morning. Wait for Jarvis. He seems to know what to do.'

Then, settling my hat again I walked swiftly across the floor and went out on to the porch. I could swear that I heard her whisper a word I'd never heard a woman use before.

'That didn't take long,' Old Billy said, looking up at me from his cards as I went into the bunkhouse.

'There wasn't anything wrong that I could fix.'

Billy didn't respond for a minute. He placed a black six on the seven of hearts and muttered, 'Remember what I said about your horse, Ryan.'

Lying on my bunk I did remember and I gave it some thought. I also remembered Art Lennox and what I owed him, Alton McCallister and what he owed me. I would stay where I was for the time being. I could risk nine more days.

Or so I thought.

SIX

Morning dawned clear and cold. Billy had been up before me firing up the stove to make pancakes, and so the bunkhouse was warm. Nevertheless we both kept our blankets wrapped around us as we ate and drank some strong coffee.

I walked outside, stretched and looked to the northern skies. It would hold clear for that day at least. I was tired of walking so I fetched my black horse from the corral and put his blanket and saddle on. He didn't mind on this morning. Standing out in the corral on the previous bitter night wasn't the same as sleeping in Givens's warm stable. He was glad to be moving, recirculating his blood and stretching his muscles. I found a patch of grass near where I hoped to be by noon, kicked away some snow to give him the idea of how to find more, and got back to fencing.

The sun rode higher in the sky as the hours passed, but although it promised warmth, it never quite touched my back. But I was working and my own muscles were warm with blood as I dug through the frost to the clean dark earth beneath and set my posts. Now and then I would look toward the house, wondering when Art would get back from another of his benders, but I saw no sign of movement. The same deer looked at me from near the creek and danced away again; the same raven – I guessed – watched me from the hummock, making hoarse comments. The black horse, unconcerned, nibbled at the sparse tufts of grass, seldom lifting his head. It was a lonesome day, I suppose, but I liked it. I liked the thunk and bite of steel from my digging bar against the cold earth and the occasional setting of new posts. I was even looking forward to the time when I had finished that and could begin to string new taut wire. I don't mind working when I can see the point in it; I don't mind being alone if that's what is needed.

I hummed old hymns that I didn't know the words to and thought of my tattered past and the new life I was going to have in Oregon. I suppose I romanticized both to fit my own specifications.

Shortly before noon I saw the three of them riding out toward the fence line.

Art Lennox was the one in front. Even at a distance I could see that he was set purposefully. Beside and a little behind him was his wife, not riding sidesaddle, but astride in a gray dress, her mouth tight, her hair escaping its pins. The third man I didn't know. He wore twin Colts and a black hat tugged low over his eyes. The pinto pony between his legs looked weary. He had a swooping

dark mustache and a pointed chin and dead eyes.
I figured this had to be Henry Jarvis. Time proved
this to be an accurate guess.

I stood with my seven-foot iron digging bar in
my hand, awaiting their arrival. The raven left with
a hasty croak. The black horse lifted its head and
watched with curiosity as the incoming riders,
moving fast and hard, approached.

They reined up sharply in front of me. Art
Lennox spoke from his lathered horse's back. He
tried to steel his words, but they came out thin and
reedy. His wife looked at me as if she had caught
someone in her pantry. Jarvis had a hand resting
familiarly on his right-hand gun. Veronica had a
shotgun lying across the withers of her pale pony.
I thought she looked the most dangerous of them
all.

'We need to talk,' Art Lennox said.

'Go ahead,' I replied. Looking from Jarvis to Art
and his wife in turn, I wondered if this had something to do with the night before. Old Billy had
been right in his appraisal of the situation, it
seemed, but unwilling to say anything blatantly. I
understood that. He needed his job, such as it was.
The West was not full of opportunities for 70-year-
old ranch hands wishing to start over.

'Just shoot him, Art,' Jarvis offered, and I braced
myself, shifting the digging bar to my other hand.
'It'll save us time.'

'Be quiet, Henry,' Lennox snapped. His face
had that pasty drunkard's pallor still. His hands
were shaking. Veronica's face, on the other hand,

was flushed with the cold and with apparent excitement. Her eyes, so warm and lovely in the firelight the night before now seemed feverish and hostile.

'Tell me what's going on, Art,' I said, and he leaned forward to talk to me. The wind shifted his pony's mane and the animal shuddered. 'Have I done something?'

'Not to me,' Lennox answered. 'Jarvis here just brought me back from town.'

'Yes. I understood that was one of his jobs,' I said, and Veronica's back stiffened.

'Well, Marshal Coombs had a visitor before we left.'

'Yes?' I had a shadow of an idea of what was coming, and I didn't like it.

'A man rode in from Yellow Tongue,' Jarvis said harshly. 'I seems you've killed a couple of men out that way.'

'In self-defense.'

'That's for a judge to decide.'

I felt everything sliding away from me: my plans for my future in Oregon, the idea of taking Ben Comfrey's pay to his wife to help her through the winter. Alton McCallister would make sure that I was tried for the shootings – he would make sure that I was hanged for them. I saw no indication of charity in Jarvis's hard eyes, none in those of Veronica Lennox. Her husband might have given me a minute to try to explain things, but he was a weak-willed man and I knew there wouldn't be any conversation about guilt or innocence.

'There's a reward out on you. The railroad's

posted it,' Jarvis said. His hand hadn't drifted far from his holster. 'It's a dead or alive sheet – murderers are always posted that way.'

I looked to Jarvis for one last chance. 'Art, I didn't do those things.' He looked away and said to no one, 'The reward is five hundred dollars. A lot of money.'

'More than a man's life is worth?' I asked.

'You don't know how much we need that money,' Veronica said with a tongue like a razor. 'Besides, we don't even know who you are. What you are. You might kill us all in our sleep, given the chance.'

'What is Coombs doing?' I asked. I wondered that they had not brought the marshal with them. 'Where is he?'

'Out looking for you. I told him you and I had parted ways after we left New Madrid. I gave him the idea that you were riding south,' Art said, without apparent shame. 'The marshal isn't allowed to collect a reward, you know ... and we need it badly.'

'That's enough chatter,' Jarvis said. 'We don't need to explain ourselves to a killer. Ryan, I'd advise you to unbuckle your gunbelt and raise your hands. You can't win.'

Before he had finished speaking, he drew his own sidearm. Before he had finished drawing it, I had shot him through the shoulder. He yelled, threw his hands out crazily and cursed loudly. His horse danced away in panic. Jarvis bounced from the saddle and landed on his head. I guessed his neck was broken. He lay still against the cold earth.

Art drew his own pistol shakily. His face told me he didn't really want any part in this, but he was a man with a gun and I treated him as such. I whipped the seven-foot digging iron against his elbow, hearing bone crack. He groaned and sagged in the saddle, dropping his revolver.

Veronica shrilled like a crazed Fury and raised her shotgun. The first load of buckshot missed me, boring a ragged hole into the earth near my foot. At the sudden confusion of sounds, her horse bucked solidly wishing to escape, and she was thrown from his back to land on her rump, the shotgun flying free of her grip.

She sat in the mud screaming and cursing as I strode toward her, picked up the shotgun and heaved it toward the creek beyond.

'You'll die!' she yelled at my back.

'So will we all one day,' I said. Then I walked to where the puzzled black horse stood watching, tightened the twin cinches on my Texas-rigged saddle and swung aboard.

I rode south then, letting the black pick its way daintily across the railroad tracks and continued on for three or four miles before I lost myself in the pine woods there. Then I swung down and rested myself against the side of my pony. My legs were trembling and I had to remove my borrowed hat and wipe the sweat from my eyes.

After a while I started on, looping through the snowy woods until I was riding north again, back toward New Madrid, back toward whatever lay beyond. At times I hate this stubborn streak in me; it seems a little like madness.

Nevertheless, these people had challenged me, had tried to arrest me, kill me, have me hanged for a series of events not of my making. I was supposed to be frightened. I was supposed to be intimidated – and I was, some. No matter. A man does what he has to do, what is right. I would prove my point, or I would die trying – unfortunately that seemed the more likely outcome, and as the cold wind from the north grew stronger, I shivered in my coat and tugged my hat lower.

I longed for Oregon.

I had already decided what I was going to do. I couldn't wait nine days for Alton McCallister to return on his train. The longer I remained in the area the more certain it would become that Marshal Coombs would find me. I had no desire to be hanged.

I was going after McCallister once again, return-ing to the Yellow Tongue Gorge. People might have thought me crazy, tracking down the man who had accused me of murder, but what else was there to do? Oregon sounded fine, but without food and supplies, I was not going to make it in the winter. No one crosses the Rockies that time of year unprepared.

There was that and the gnawing guilt about deserting Ben Comfrey's wife to the rigors of winter. She would be lucky if she could make it to springtime without help. And – McCallister owed me more than that. He owed me an apology and needed to stand up and admit he was lying about what I had done to him personally.

The other charges had no bases in fact. Whether I could clear all of that up was doubtful, but I could straighten out the charges between the law and myself where McCallister was concerned. Or so I hoped. I wanted to extract a written promise from him that he would deny his allegations.

And I wanted that $149.00.

I guess to some rich man it might sound foolish to be willing to die for that kind of money, but I figure when a man works for you he has a contract. He has given his word as his bond and to refuse a worker his honest pay is to break that bond. It is dishonest; it is cheating and lying. And to withhold it from a widow after her husband has died trying to provide – that goes beyond despicable. Civilized countries for thousands of years have had special statutes in law protecting widows and orphans. Well, I was the law now, there being no other willing to act.

With the bright shining of a new day after one more frozen night, I continued westward. I could follow the railroad tracks without riding too near by the glint of the sun on the new steel of the rails. I came upon a herd of about forty elk that morning, majestically antlered old bucks, does and fawns. They hardly paid attention to me. I think I could have ridden through the herd without disturbing them. They had never seen a man, it seemed, and it could have been so. That would change when the railroad locomotives became a permanent fixture in their wild range, spewing smoke and clattering along the tracks.

Had I been traveling free and easy I would have considered taking down one of the bull elks for meat. I could have eaten for weeks off the steaks. However, now was hardly the time to unlimber my rifle or stop to butcher and smoke the meat.

Marshal Coombs was back there and he would still be trying to track me, and with snow still on the ground, he and his posse would eventually cut my sign. It was ironic, but Jarvis and Veronica had actually done me a favor by lying to the marshal about the direction I had taken.

Maybe now – with any sort of luck – I could finish what had to be done before lighting out for Oregon again.

The Yellow Tongue Gorge, when I found it, looked as deeply shadowed, raw and rugged as it had before. Snowmelt ran down the flanks of the great canyon, and the trestle I saw from a distance, had nearly been completed. Maybe the arrival of the railroad manager had speeded the building of the spiderwork of timbers.

I sat my black horse half a mile away, watching the scene. I noted a few men, ant-like at that distance, crawling up the framework of the trestle, saw a tree felled unexpectedly, the crack as its trunk shattered clear across the cold distances. The slopes had been nearly denuded now.

And there was the train. The black locomotive was inert on the tracks, the Pullmans like segments of a giant insect still and motionless. There was a dusting of snow on their roofs. There was no movement within or around them that I could make out. Where were all the pretty ladies, I wondered?

Where was Alton McCallister?

I could just make out the pay office, looking small and humble. The long barracks emitted a thin drift of smoke; the stable was squat and bereft of activity. I thought how small all human endeavors looked when seen from a distance.

I swung down from the back of my weary horse, loosened the cinches and squatted on my heels. I glanced to the skies and saw that day had not long to live before it flared with red and orange and died away to purple death. I also considered that this could be my last day on earth before I faded away into some unknown twilight passage. I didn't like that idea and chased it from my mind and used the gloaming time to clean my guns and make my plans.

I was at least on familiar ground, having spent the end of summer and autumn in the lumber camp. The night was dark, sheathing me in invisibility, and my boots made only a soft crunching sound against the snow. The wind, while active, was still far from cold. I could pick out the lights of the individual buildings – stable, bunkhouse, office, supply shed – and oriented myself immediately. I was alert for roaming guards, but I didn't think they could have predicted my unannounced arrival here where the danger was most immediate. Nevertheless, I moved carefully and swiftly, darting from shadow to shadow among the scattered pine and cedar trees. There is always danger when a man moves among the guns.

Pausing on the northern flank of a low knoll, I searched the camp and the perimeter before focusing on my objective. The huge black form of the 4-4-2 locomotive and its silent Pullman appendages was no more than fifty yards below. Now there were lights on in both passenger cars and I saw movement behind the screened windows. Yet the wind swept away all sound and I might have been on the moon for all of the signs of life.

I started down toward the head of the locomotive, eyes constantly searching. Once, across the distances, I heard a crash and a muffled curse – noises, I assumed, emanating from the bunkhouse where some of the boys would now be finishing off their day with raw whiskey.

Moving in a crouch, I slid up beside the locomotive over the blue snow. The moon was an eerie visitor above me, peering at intervals through the fragmented clouds. I rested a hand against the cold flank of the iron horse as I caught my breath and decided on my next move.

There were gold painted curlicues and whimsical striping decorating the big engine. Even the huge drive wheels were painted with filigree. The brass bell shone like a bit of bright pride in the starlight. It was a great iron animal waiting to have its heart stoked with fire and begin its powerful run across the plains.

I slipped toward the rear of the locomotive,

passed the coal tender and swiftly climbed the iron ladder at the front of the first Pullman. I knew from my last visit that the car in the rear was where they held their parties and played at cards; that the front car was reserved for sleeping and dressing.

I mounted to the roof of the Pullman and quickly went to my belly. There was a moving shadow on the ground near me, a watchman with a Winchester repeater in his hand. I lay there against the cold roof of the Pullman, trying to still my breath as the man – wearing a long buffalo coat – walked past me slowly, in no hurry to get anywhere. He didn't seem to be particularly alert, which suited me fine. If he had raised his eyes once he could have seen me on top of the train and easily drilled me where I lay.

He strode on. I thought I could hear a faint, tuneless whistle escaping his lips.

I stayed on my belly, inching ahead until I reached the rear of the car, then hastily I swung down, burst into the lighted Pullman and came face to face with the guard Tom. His eyes opened wide in total surprise and I clubbed him with the barrel of my Colt. He sagged to the floor of the corridor. I looked into a nearby compartment, found it empty and dragged Tom into it.

I was sweating now. Iron stoves heated the car and the difference between indoor and outdoor temperatures was extreme. I went on.

I opened the door to the next compartment carefully and by the dim light of a lantern saw a young good-looking woman lying in bed, her dark hair free of its pins. She saw me too. She drew the blankets up to just below her wide eyes. I smiled at her and put a finger to my lips. She didn't scream or move an inch as I backed from the room.

Next door I found my man.

I slipped inside, halting Alton McCallister in the motion of lighting a cigar. He sat in a luxurious green velvet-covered chair, his polished boots propped up on the bed. He wore a pair of black trousers and a cream-colored shirt, the top button undone, tie loose around his neck. He scowled at me and lowered his cigar. Green eyes examined me from beneath his reddish eyebrows. He touched a finger to his mustache and spoke firmly.

'What are you trying to do, Ryan? Commit suicide?'

'I am trying,' I told him, as I closed the door and leaned a shoulder against it, 'to collect the pay due me and my friend.'

'If you'd been out working – all the time you've put into this charade – you could have more than made up the money.'

'That isn't the point,' I said. My throat was a little dry. I felt more nervous than McCallister looked. 'The point is that you owe the money. Ben was killed by your men.'

'This is all merely a point of honor?'

'That's all it is, McCallister. Pay me and I'll leave you alone. I sure don't want to see you ever again.' My Colt, held loosely by my thigh now rose and he glanced at it.

'All right,' he said after a slow minute. 'I'll agree

with you on this – this has gone quite far enough.'

Slowly he lowered his cigar and placed it on the table. Then he got to his feet and removed a purse from a drawer. I warned him with a gesture and the cocking of my pistol that there had better not be a weapon hidden there and he smiled thinly, acknowledging the silent command. When he turned he opened the chamois purse and removed a handful of gold eagles, scattering them on the table in bright disarray.

'I don't want all of it,' I said, shaking my head. I didn't want anyone coming back to say I had robbed the railroad boss at gunpoint. 'You owe me a hundred and forty-nine dollars.' Having said that, I carefully counted out seven twenty-dollar double-eagles and one ten-dollar piece. 'I'll send you the change.

'Sit down,' I ordered.

'I thought you said that this was all you wanted,' McCallister said, but he sat down and raised his hands to shoulder level.

'It is. I'm taking this gold and disappearing. I don't want to ever see you again; I want no further trouble. Be big enough to swallow it and stay out of my tracks. I'm not looking back, McCallister. I hope you won't either.

'Next time,' I added, more angrily, 'I might have to do something both of us will regret.' Pocketing the coins I backed through the door. 'I know you're not a stupid man, McCallister, but I should warn you – don't poke your head out into the corridor.' He eyed my Colt once more and nodded. I could see anger burning in his eyes, but there was nothing I could do about that. I started quickly toward the rear platform, not wanting Tom to wake up before I was well away from the train.

Some impulse caused me to pause along the carpeted aisle and again open the door where the woman had been abed. She was still sitting up, still holding her blankets in front of her, still watching with huge saucer eyes.

'It's all right,' I told her. 'I'm leaving now. You're safe.'

For a second I thought she was going to scream, that I had made an incredibly stupid, clumsy mistake of gallantry. Her lips parted, forming a rouged oval around her small white teeth. Then she relaxed her mouth and closed it. Her hands trembled still. But just for a moment I thought I caught the beginnings of a smile in her eyes.

McCallister's voice suddenly rang out and I hightailed it for the rear platform. He must have seen the guard walking his rounds and called out the window to alert him because when I reached the rear of the Pullman I came face to face with the guard.

He raised his rifle and fired at what would have been a dead shot at point-blank range except I had been a little quicker and threw myself from the platform to land rolling in the snow. The landing was a rough one, and it knocked the wind out of me.

Without light, the guard couldn't find me immediately for a second shot. I drew my pistol and fired

86

wildly three times. I know I missed because I heard the sharp ricochets of lead ringing off steel. Then I saw the muzzle flash of the railroad guard's Winchester and heard the simultaneous boom of the .44.40. Flame flashed from his muzzle and I knew that it had been another close call.

Breathing well or not, I made a run for it and I darted across the snowy expanse of the open ground, weaving as I went. Two more shots were fired in my direction before I was lost in darkness. I tripped and sat down hard, fumbling with my cartridge belt, trying to reload with shaking hands.

A shout had gone up from near the barracks and I saw a dozen or so lumberjacks and steel drivers swarm out into the night, silhouetted by the light in the doorway behind them. Someone unlimbered a rifle and aimed a shot at me that went wide, but not wide enough. I came to my knee and emptied my revolver in their direction. I hit no one, but they yelped, cursed and rushed back into the barracks, to collect boots, coats and weapons, I guessed.

Shoving more cartridges into the cylinder of my Colt Army I rose to my feet and legged it out of there. If they reappeared with rifles, I was in for it. The distance to the barracks was no more than fifty yards. Not much range for a good sharpshooter with a rifle, but a lot of distance for a running man with only a handgun in his arsenal.

I plunged on through the snow. The skies held clear, too clear for my purposes and I ran until my lungs were burning and my heart racing madly. Men had now emerged from the Pullman cars and from the office. They were all shouting contradictory orders, and some of them began to fire wildly, wanting to be in on the kill. I had never seen it happen before, but it happened to me then: a bullet from one of the rifles tagged my gunhand and the Colt went spinning from my grip. It stunned my hand as if someone had struck me with a sledgehammer. I had instant numbness from my fingertips to my shoulder. The following pain was violent and heavy. Still, I told myself, it might have been my hand that went spinning off. I should count myself lucky.

I scrambled across the snow on hands and knees, searching for my pistol, knowing it was a lost cause. By then every employee of the railroad and all of McCallister's friends seemed to be bearing down on me with angry guns. I didn't choose to be shot or hanged. There were flaring torches and a lot of curse-filled exchanges. I looked to the pine woods where I had left my horse and started that way at a run, my arm dangling uselessly.

Once they found my tracks they would have no trouble trailing me in the snow, even in these conditions. Fortunately I had yet to see a following man on horseback. They hadn't, in their mad rush to kill me, taken the time to get to the stable and saddle their ponies, so I still had a chance.

I was sure they could run me to ground in a matter of minutes. I was just as sure there wasn't a man alive who could outrace my black gelding. I reached the woods, chest and arm aching. I nearly collided with a huge pine in the darkness the forest provided. For a moment I panicked – I was sure that I had left the black tethered to a massive cedar; I was sure it was just to my right, to the west, but I did not see it standing there.

I raced on. Abruptly the horse appeared in silhouette, starlight glinting on the whites of his eyes. I started the horse running almost before I was mounted and wove madly through the dark woods. Behind me there were a few shots, then the curses grew fainter and slowly receded as the black horse covered the distance before me.

I did not slow for hours. I didn't know if by now they had saddled their horses and were in pursuit. In the starlight my horse's tracks still stood out plainly.

I picked out the Dipper over my left shoulder and began riding east. It was back toward where Marshal Coombs was presumably still on the look-out for me, but that couldn't be helped. Riding south I might have had a chance of making a clean getaway. North to Canada also offered a chance of escape. The Rockies looming to the west, stagger-ing the eye with their 14,000-foot high peaks, were far too formidable for a man riding equipped as I was at this time of year. Oregon would have to wait again.

None of these considerations determined my course. I had made a promise to a young woman I had never seen and her dead husband, to myself. I was riding to Billings with Ben Comfrey's money for his widow to try to make it through a hard winter.

SEVEN

Hours passed slowly and it only grew colder as I rode on through the bitter night. My horse held his head low and I sagged in the saddle. I glanced at the stars again to take my bearings and noticed the haze around them. Like thin fog, some disguise of nature. It took me a minute to understand what I was seeing.

Wafer-thin drifting clouds had begun to frost the stars and cover them. I swung my head around and looked to the north. There, by the scant moonlight, I saw the sky was ominous, heavily stacked and moving toward me quickly. Lightning crackled and there was the rumble of following distant thunder. By the pale flash of the distant web of lightning, I could see more clearly that the storm was progressing with savage intensity. I picked up my weary horse's pace, but it was futile, of course – we were not going to outrun the driving storm.

The wind grew heavy on my back and the sky fell to complete darkness. The first snow began to fall within the hour. I had no idea where I was. I knew of no shelter for miles and miles around me. I bowed my head once more and urged the exhausted black on. Soon the darkness and the smothering snowfall obliterated all vision. There was only the snow and the dark of the freezing night. I could see nothing. If I were to ride off a cliff I could have done nothing. My eyes were tightly closed and now I could feel ice forming on my lashes. I tied my bandanna over nose and mouth to try warming the lung-freezing air.

The horse plodded on, perhaps moving in a slow circle. There was no telling. I was completely lost. I remembered a tale I had heard of fifty Dakota schoolchildren lost in such a storm. They had all become disoriented and frozen to death, some within fifty feet of their cabins while anxious parents stood in the doorways, banging spoons on iron pots, hoping to guide them home.

I thought of that tragedy and then I recalled a night in Denver when I had filled a straight and won $200 in gold from ... what had the man's name been? There was a woman with him. She seemed to have been a friend of mine. The man laughed a lot and smoked big cigars. *My Aunt Hanna had never trusted men who smoked cigars.* I shook my head; it did no good. It was encased in ice. *My dog's name was Willie ... there was something the matter with one of his eyes ...* my thoughts such as they were, revolved, spun madly around my skull and then went black.

I found myself lying in the snow. My horse was

92

not there, or if it was, I could not see it. I looked upward. I knew it was up because that was where the driving snow fell from. I didn't feel so cold now. I just felt like sleeping. Death, I thought, was not that bad at all once your teeth quit chattering and the flow of blood simply ceased.

The first thing they tried to feed me was a kind of broth made from the marrow of an elk's bones and Indian potatoes. I couldn't swallow it although it was warm and I needed warmth badly. I finally clawed my eyes open and discovered where I was. A shallow cave with a rough floor was glowing dully in the smoky light cast by the damp burning wood in a small fire ring. I could see the opening of the cave and the unrelenting snow falling beyond it.

I was surrounded by four Cheyenne Indians, watching me with dark eyes. Two of them were men of forty or more years, one an ancient woman, one a very young boy wrapped to his eyes in striped blankets. I tried to sit up, could not. One of the men came to me, lifted my eyelids and propped me up against the cold stone of the cave wall. Then he again offered me a bowlful of broth. There was nothing in their expressions as I greedily swallowed the warm soup. After a few swallows, I immediately went back to sleep.

It must have been two hours later when I awoke again and sat up on my own, feeling that I might somehow survive the night now. Again they gave me some of the broth and I drank it greedily. The firelight danced against the walls of the cave and across the faces of the Indians. One of the men wore his hair in two braids, the other had his loose across his shoulders. The flickering firelight cast moving shadows. One of the men, I saw, had an angry scar running the length of his face on the right side, a savage cut that had narrowly avoided his eye. The old woman looked down at her work-thickened hands, not glancing up. The boy peered at me from beneath his blanket and I smiled and winked at him. There was absolutely no response. Tiredly I placed the bowl aside and then lay down again. I was instantly asleep.

When I awoke next it was to the glare of brilliant sunlight on new snow visible beyond the mouth of the cave. The sky above was a clear deep blue as if it had never stormed at all. Something nudged my foot and I turned my head.

My black horse was there, tethered to a stone fallen from the roof of the cave. The Cheyenne were gone. Embers still burned in the fire ring but there was no other sign that they had even been there. I stood shakily and walked to the cave opening to look out at the new morning. Not a sign of passing marred the surface of the new fallen snow. The Indians had simply vanished like the wind-driven clouds.

I walked to my horse, rubbing its neck. I was amazed to find it there. Somehow the Indians had caught it up and brought it here for me. I knew that the animal would have been very valuable to them, but they had not taken it.

I checked the saddle-bags and found nothing

taken from them either. I didn't know who those wandering people were or where they were traveling; I could only wish them well on the trail. The hat Old Billy had given me was there, crushed in my saddle-bags. I formed it roughly with my hands and put it on. Also in the saddle-bags was Ben Comfrey's gun and gunbelt. I checked over the revolver and then holstered it. It was loaded, but not in great shape.

The blue steel Colt had once been a fine gun, better than any I had owned. It had mother-of-pearl handgrips, one of them chipped slightly. It had been a long time since Ben had wiped off the pistol when it was wet or oiled it when it was dry, but it would have to do. I untethered the black and walked it to the cave entrance, its steel-shod hoofs clicking against the stone. I stood there for quite a few minutes, just studying the land before me. Then I led the horse outside and swung aboard, riding eastward toward Billings once more.

The hours passed in weary progression. A tired horse carrying a tired man toward some inexact destination across the long prairie. I was hungry again, naturally. I did spy a small group of antelope near a narrow rill, but as hungry as I was it didn't seem like a good idea to fire my rifle and butcher and cook some meat. I saw no one for miles, but a rifle shot would roll a long way across this silent landscape. Smoke would be a dead giveaway as well. I decided to travel hungry but alive.

There was a dull orange glow to the western sky and the dying sun was painting the snowdrifts with violet shadows when I topped a low rise and saw lights burning in the distance. There were more than a few of them, clustered together. It could not be a ranch; I took it for Billings. Even if it wasn't, I could nevertheless find some kind of shelter and food for the black horse and myself. I didn't pause to enjoy the view. I kept on my way and before the last glow of sundown had faded from the skies I found myself riding a muddy rutted road that ran straight ahead of me through the town. I could see little enough of the town in the dusk, but I passed a dry goods store with a false front and across this was emblazoned BILLINGS EMPORIUM. So I had found my way after all.

Two boys, about twelve years old, came racing down the boardwalk, coats flapping, scarves around their necks. They were wasting no time – late for supper, I figured.

'Hey, where's a stable?' I called out, and the larger of the two pointed up the street without pausing to speak. Two ruddy-faced men sat behind a long desk inside the stable proper. They showed no undue interest as I swung down and loosened the weary black's saddle cinches. I walked to the desk.

One of the men – they seemed to be brothers, both with heavy cheeks and mournful watery eyes – was biting on the stub of a pencil, moving his lips as he studied the list of figures and notations before him. Settling accounts. The other one, his red plaid shirt sleeves rolled up to reveal work-smudged long johns, watched me thoughtfully and asked, 'Want to put your horse up?' He spoke mechanically, his voice deep and solid. I nodded in response. 'How long you planning on keeping him here, and what do you want him fed? Fifty cents a day is the going rate.' He spoke as if it was a constantly recited speech, and probably it was. His brother, if that was who it was, never looked up. Now he made a mark with a pencil and frowned, pushing out his lower lip.

'Just overnight,' I said. 'I want him given new hay – no straw – and oats if you have them.'

'Oats are extra.'

I nodded. 'I figured as much.' His eyes continued to study me thoughtfully. I wasn't entirely presentable and I knew what he wanted to ask. I managed to open my purse quite casually and make sure he caught a glimpse of the gold coins there. 'I'll have to get change. I'll be back tomorrow.'

'I know you will,' the stableman answered. 'That is, unless you want to lose a fine-looking animal like that over so little money.' Now he did smile and I returned it. We understood each other.

'Rub him down well, will you?' I asked. 'He's had a long ride.'

He might have been wishing to ask me where I had ridden in from, but neither of these two seemed concerned with idle conversation.

'Do you know a man named Ben Comfrey, lived around here?' I enquired.

'Seems I've heard the name,' he said, with a heavy shake of his bullish head, 'but I don't know him. At least, he's done no business with us. Know the name, Chesty?' he asked his partner.

'No!' the one called Chesty said angrily, then he got back to laboriously balancing his accounts. I had the idea that adding and subtracting didn't come easy for him.

My horse settled into a stall, I went out into the cold night. Frost streamed from my lips as I walked the boardwalk, my boot-heels clicking on the weathered wood. I passed two saloons and considered going in. Someone was bound to know where Ben Comfrey's place was. Just then, however, I didn't care to be observed. It was possible that word of me, a wanted poster had made it to Billings by now. For one night I wanted to be warm, well fed and comfortable. The hotel I found seemed substantial and clean enough and I entered, looking around.

The hotel had an adjacent restaurant. Looking through the batwing door that separated the two, I could see men and ladies enjoying their meals. I could smell steak and yams, cornbread. The desk clerk signed me in almost without looking at me. He was busy arguing with a handyman about something he had not done to repair the shingle roof over the kitchen. 'I'm going to have to let you go if you can't do no better, Earl,' he said to a rough-looking man who smirked in response as if it made no difference to him either way. I paid no attention, signed the book with my head down and ordered a meal to be brought to my room.

'I'm too dirty and too tired for a restaurant just

now,' I explained, and that much was true.

I climbed the stairs almost unnoticed and found my room. Opening it I went in. There was a large bed, somewhat sagging, with a thick comforter spread on it. I tossed my hat on to the bedpost, tugged off my travel-encrusted boots and lay back on the bed, hands clasped behind my head, studying the ceiling. Within minutes, a slender kid of eighteen or so knocked at my door and I let him enter and place my dinner tray on the low bureau beside the window.

When he had gone, I turned the brass key in the lock and pulled the room's single chair to the dresser, sat, eyed the thick steak I had ordered with reverence and picked up knife and fork to go at it. I ate everything on the tray, drank a cup of coffee and tucked my weary body in bed beneath the thick comforter. The bed was soft, the room warm. I was away from the ice and snow of the plains. There was nothing more a man could want. I yawned twice, stretched once and dropped into a dreamless sleep.

I thought I would sleep for a long time, but I awoke before dawn and rose from my bed to cross the room. I stood looking out the window at the black distances where only a few scattered, feeble lights glowed. I thought about slipping out of town before sunrise, but decided against it. Then I thought of Ben Comfrey's wife out there alone in some small house with her supplies running down to nothing with winter barely begun. After that it was impossible to go back to sleep and so I slowly washed off with a bar of soap and towel left beside the basin, dusted off my clothing and boots as well as I could with a provided whiskbroom, and dressed as dawn began to spread its hueless early light across the eastern sky.

I drifted downstairs, seeing no one else about. A desk clerk – a different man from the night before, slept, tilted back in a wooden chair behind the counter. Beyond the batwing doors I could smell coffee boiling in the restaurant. I walked through to seat myself. There was only one other customer – a lonesome, weary-looking man who might have been a buffalo hunter or mountain man driven down from the high reaches by the snow. He looked up at me with red eyes, nodded and returned his gaze to his coffee mug which he was cupping with both hands for its warmth.

A bright-eyed, sassy-looking girl appeared from the kitchen with a handful of silverware, glanced at me, put the silverware down and wiped her hands on her short apron.

'What'll you have?' she asked brightly.

'What's the cook got up? I'll take anything that you can bring me soon.'

'He's ready to go with anything,' she said. 'Ham's sliced, hotcake batter's mixed, griddles hot and we got eggs.'

'Some of each,' I told her, 'and coffee.'

'You got it,' she said. I wondered how anyone could be so perky at this hour, but she was. She scribbled something down on her pad and started away, but I stopped her before she could leave.

'Do you happen to know a man named Ben Comfrey?' I asked, and I described him briefly as she shook her head doubtfully.

' 'Fraid not,' she said. Someone's voice – the cook's, I supposed, called out from the kitchen.

'Myrtle!'

'Shut up,' she said under her breath, looking that way. To me, she said, 'I don't know the man, sorry, mister,' and scurried away again.

Two men in heavy sheepskin coats entered, looked around and stamped to a corner table. I looked away from them, not knowing if there might not be a star hidden beneath those coats. When I looked back the older man with the tangled gray-streaked hair, the one I had taken for a buffalo hunter, was standing next to my table.

'Mind if I sit down?' he asked. His hands, I noticed, were trembling. They were big-veined and gnarled. His red eyes had a deep sadness in them. I shrugged and he slid a chair out from the table. Myrtle had returned with a pot of coffee and she looked at him and then at me. I made a small gesture to indicate that it was all right. If I read the man across from me correctly he had no money for breakfast and perhaps none even to pay for the coffee he had been nursing so carefully.

'You want anything to eat?' I offered, and we called Myrtle back. After ordering, he cleared his throat drily and said, 'I heard you asking about Ben Comfrey.'

'Do you know him?'

'Yes, I do! One of the biggest-hearted men I've

met. Last winter he let me hole up in his haybarn for three months. Never asked me for anything but a bit of handy work. My name's Pez. Pez Traylor,' he said, offering me his hand. 'I was trapping in the high country. Beaver.' He shook his head. 'They seem mainly to be trapped out now, though. It's a shame.

'But I came down with a fair take, not wanting to winter up there. First thing I know I got robbed on the trail by three men. Two Crow warriors and a white man. They took my skins and left me there with nothing, not even my mule. By the time I reached Billings I was near froze, half starved.

'Ben Comfrey, he heard my hard luck story and let me stay with him. A man with a big heart.'

'He was,' I agreed.

'You know Ben, then. . . .' He hesitated. 'Wait, what do you mean he *was?*'

'He and I went timbering for the railroad. He got killed,' I had to tell him.

'Killed. . . .' The old man's face showed concern followed by bewilderment and then anger. 'Someone murdered him?'

'I'm afraid so.'

'Well, damn!' His hands clenched. I had the idea that the trapper had been hoping to winter up once more at Ben's farm. His head shifted slightly with what might have been despair. We removed our arms from the table as Myrtle set our plates down then scurried away to start teasing and flirting with the men in the sheepskin coats whom she seemed to know well.

'That's going to be hell on his wife.' Pez looked at me more deeply. 'Is that what you came here for, to tell her that Ben's dead?'

'Yes.'

'I don't envy you that task. I always hate that task.'

I didn't say a word about the money I had for her. In general it's better not to talk about money with someone you don't know, especially when he looks like someone who could use a little of it himself. I liked Pez, thought he was probably sincere, hopefully honest – but you just never knew.

He fell to eating with ravenous appetite and I wasn't far behind him. When we were down to coffee and empty platters, I said, 'You can tell me where Ben's place is, then?'

'Sure. I'll draw you a little map though it ain't hard to find.' He considered silently and then added, 'Do you want me to ride out there with you?'

'No, it's better that I do it alone,' I answered, without giving my reasons.

'I understand.' After a minute's reflection, he added, 'I guess that's it for me, then. Truth is,' he told me with a sad smile that revealed broken teeth, 'I was kinda hoping to stay there again this winter. Truth is – and I hate to admit it – I'm too old for trapping, too old for the snow and the high mountain struggle.'

I didn't answer, just gave a commiserating nod. Pez said, 'This knocks the chocks from under my wheels. Can't expect a widow to take me in and feed me for free.'

'No,' I was forced to agree.

'Well,' he said with false brightness, 'maybe I can find some handyman work around town.' His eyes weren't touched by this surge of optimism. It seemed a long shot, but I offered one idea.

'Why don't you talk to the people at the hotel, Pez? They just might have an opening for someone who can patch a split-shingle roof.'

'Think so?'

'Something I heard,' I shrugged. 'I wouldn't know for sure. Anyway, it's worth a try.'

'Yes, it's that. You know, I didn't get your name,' he said.

'Ryan. Just Ryan.'

We shook hands again and he rose. 'Well, I thank you for the suggestion, and thank you again for the meal. Let me draw you a little map here of how to find old Ben's place,' he said, setting about it with a stubby pencil and a scrap of paper. 'I don't envy you your task, Ryan,' he said once more with a shake of his head. 'I surely do not.'

I was unhappy with my lot as well, but I had come a long way and gone through much to do what had to be done. After settling up my bills all around, I started the black down the trail in the grimly brilliant light of the new morning. There was still a hint of violet and of rose in the eastern sky, but the sunlight was brilliant off the snow and I tugged down my hat and squinted my eyes as I rode on.

*

The homestead Ben Comfrey had been so proud of wasn't much to see. Low sod house and flimsy barn. I saw a few cattle dotted here and there about the place foraging for something to nibble at and two horses in a pole corral around back. The cottonwood trees were sparse and gray in the cold daylight. The high sun showed me an acre or so where wheat had been planted. The crop looked withered and mostly flattened, bent by the wind and snow of the past week.

A single leafless elm stood beside the narrow front porch of the house, and a yellow hound came out to meet me as I approached the soddy, waggling its tail, its belly low to the ground, unsure how to approach me.

It hadn't been much of a place in the best of times, now it looked ready to crumble and fade back into the prairie. But Ben had spoken glowingly of it. A man's home, a man's woman is always the most beautiful to him. I swung down from the black and tied it loosely to the hitch rail.

I removed my hat, wiped back my hair and stood watching the house uncertainly. All was quiet. I began to step up on to the sagging porch when I saw the door open a few inches, hesitantly, shyly.

'Who are you?' a woman's voice asked, her voice quavering.

'Is this the Comfrey place?'

'Who are you? Who wants to know?'

'I was a friend of Ben's. I have some of his things.'

There was a long, heavy silence and then I heard the woman say, 'I knew he was dead. I knew it. He promised he'd be back before the first snow fell. And he never came.'

The door opened fully and a small woman with dark gold hair emerged. She wore a shawl and she kept it against her with crossed arms. It was the woman I had seen in the picture, no doubt of it, but she was no slip of a girl now, but a mature, handsome female. She stepped nearer to me, looking down at my face. The wind twisted a loose strand of hair across her eyes. She brushed it away wearily.

'What's your name?' she asked.

'Ryan. I worked with Ben out at the Yellow Tongue.'

She continued to eye me skeptically. 'How did you find the place?'

'A man named Pez told me how to find it.'

She nodded to herself and looked briefly skyward. Her eyes were a deep green, something I could not have guessed from the daguerreotype of her. The light wind gusted a little. A hawk screeched from somewhere above us, and she broke her silence.

'You may as well come in,' she said, with a woman's infinite sadness. She was not crying; I guessed she had already shed her tears when the crops began to wither and Ben had not arrived as he had promised.

I untied my saddle-bags, shouldered them and followed her into the low-ceilinged house. It was small and dark. Only two high, narrow windows illuminated the soddy. The packed earth floor had been swept, though, and on the mantel over the stone fireplace were three pieces of pewter and two good porcelain statuettes. I smelled coffee and cornpone. That had been her breakfast, I supposed.

'Sit down,' she said, waving a hand limply toward the table and four chairs that dominated the room. 'I'll heat the coffee.'

'Thank you.' I sat, placed my hat on the chair beside me and opened my saddle-bags, withdrawing the daguerreotype, and Ben's paybook. I sat in silence as she prodded the embers in her iron stove to life and placed the half-gallon blue coffeepot on, using her apron as a hotpad. She was trim and carried herself erectly, I noticed. A proud woman. When she turned to face me I was struck again by the deep green of her eyes. It was sad to see that they had no life in them. Her hard life had removed any sparkle they might once have held.

'You said that you have some of Ben's things.'

'Not much.' He hadn't had much. 'There's this,' I said, sliding the picture of her and the young boy across the table. She picked it up and examined it, the corner of her mouth lifting in a hint of a smile. Her eyes grew reminiscent.

'Was I ever that young?' she said to herself. The coffee began to boil and she returned to the stove to fill two white ceramic cups and brought them to the table, seating herself opposite me.

'This is what Ben wanted you to have most,' I said, and I counted out his wages in gold. 'And I brought his paybook along so that you can see that it's an accurate accounting.'

She ignored my last words and the blue paybook I placed in front of her. In a sort of angry wonder she looked at the small stack of coins I had given her. Bright gold and silver. I knew she hadn't seen that much for a long time, but she didn't seem happy.

'Is this what a man's life is worth?' she said in a muted voice, and now I did see moisture in her eyes. I looked away and took a sip of the strong hot coffee as she dabbed at her eyes with the corner of her apron. I had no answer to make.

'Ben was trying to do his best,' I said, meeting her gaze with my own. 'A man does what he can.' She remained silent. 'He was proud of you, this place, his son. He must have shown me that picture a hundred times.'

She shook her head. 'That's not Ben's son. He's my brother, Bobby.'

'Oh?'

'My father never came back from the war. Cholera took my mother. I was only sixteen when I met Ben Comfrey. He took Bobby and me both in. Ben and I didn't . . . couldn't.' Her eyes flickered and grew more intense. 'What happened to Ben, Ryan?'

'He was murdered.'

'Murdered? But who would want to kill Ben?'

I hadn't heard the door open behind me, but

now from the doorway came the accusing words, 'He killed Ben, Sis. Don't you see it? This is the man who killed Ben.'

EIGHT

I slowly shifted my eyes without moving my hands. Standing in the open doorway was a boy of fourteen or so. On the floor where he had dropped them were two dead rabbits. In his hands was a double-barreled twelve-gauge shotgun aimed carelessly at me.

'What are you talking about, Bobby?' Comfrey's wife asked, her eyes going to mine and then back to her brother's. 'Ryan just rode all the way from Yellow Tongue to bring Ben's pay to us.'

'And where did he get Ben's pay from?' the kid demanded. I didn't like the set of his full mouth nor the glint in his brownish-green eyes. 'Ask yourself that? Then ask yourself another question: why is he carrying Ben's pistol in his holster? It's Ben's,' he told her sharply, as she tried to look. 'I'd know it anywhere. He loved that pistol.'

The woman looked to me questioningly. I answered the unspoken question: 'Ben and I got into a fight with some men. He was shot and killed. I took his gun to bring to you. Later I lost my own

110

revolver so I've been carrying his ever since. If you like, I'll give it to you now.'

'Don't you be reaching for that gun!' the kid, Bobby, ordered, and I placed my hand back on the table very carefully.

'You must be wrong, Bobby,' the woman objected.

'I'm not wrong,' he said. There was nervousness in his voice, but he was resolute as well. 'And who says that's all the money Ben earned. There might be more, a lot more.'

'There's his paybook,' I said calmly. 'You can examine it.'

'I intend to. Sis, maybe he isn't a crook. Maybe he's just a killer. Maybe he and Ben scrapped and he killed Ben. Maybe his conscience got to bothering him and so he decided to bring that money here. I don't know for sure, but I don't like him being here. I say we tell him to mount up and ride. Right now!'

The woman was a long time answering. She looked again at the picture she had placed on the table before her and then gave her head a small shake.

'No, Bobby.'

'Nina!' Bobby's voice shook. He was angry, but I thought he also did not like being thwarted now that he was man of the house.

'I said "no", Bobby. We don't throw guests out at gunpoint. This man has ridden a long way to bring Ben's pay to us, and we need it sorely. We will not repay kindness with rudeness. He at least deserves our thanks and a chance to rest.' The boy stood stock-still, his mouth was slightly open. His eyes shifted from me to Nina and back. His sister said, 'Now get outside and skin those rabbits if you want them for our dinner.'

Sullenly he snatched up the rabbits and went out, throwing one last poisonous glance my way.

'I didn't come here to cause trouble,' I said. 'I can leave as soon as stay. There's no need for my presence to cause friction.' I had half-risen from my chair when she stopped me.

'No, Ryan. It's not just you, but Bobby has to learn the proper way to do things. You are a guest; our guests are to be treated with kindness.'

I sipped again at my coffee. It had grown cool in the meantime. I glanced toward the open door, seeing the bright snow surrounding scant patches of grass. I could see a corner of the wheat field with its wilted growth. Nina followed my eyes.

'I tried to reap as much as I could, but it wasn't much good even then, and the job was too much for me.' She looked at the palms of her hands and smiled distantly. 'It wouldn't have been enough to save us anyway, and the hay won't last the horses through winter, let alone the cattle. Those I shall have to sell off.'

'You'll have food at least, and come spring—'

She interrupted me. 'We won't be here come spring. I was willing to try holding out as long as Ben was here. Now . . . he's not coming back, is he?'

'What are you going to do?' I asked.

'There's a woman in town who owns a hair-dressing salon. She's getting older and needs help. There's a small apartment above the salon, large enough for Bobby and me.' She gave a small shrug. 'We can make out all right there. It's a desperate plan we've discussed already, hoping we would never have to do it. That everything would be somehow be all right once Ben returned.'

Her expression was downcast. All hope of saving the farm seemed to be gone; I could see that. I could offer no advice. 'Maybe it's for the best,' I said, for something to say. I glanced toward the door again. 'How does Bobby feel about the idea?'

'He hates it!' Nina said. 'He's a country boy. He likes to hunt and fish. He likes working in the open with no boss around watching over his shoulder. He always thought he would live on this ranch the rest of his life. That we would build it up, do all the things Ben had in mind. Build a real wood house—' Her voice broke off and again I saw a dampness in her eyes, tears she would not allow herself to shed.

She was young; I had to remind myself of that. She would be twenty-four years old now by my reckoning. Awful young to have your dreams disappear and have to give yourself up to an existence of drudgery.

She sighed audibly, rose and took our cups to the counter. 'Ben was the only father Bobby has ever known,' she said, keeping her back to me. 'I don't know if he really believes you had anything to do with Ben's death, but the news was a terrible

113

shock to him, I'm sure.'

'If I thought I could say anything to help. . . .'

'You can't. Don't try.' She stood facing away from me for another little while. I rose, putting my hat on. Nina untied her apron, folded it and offered me another of her meager smiles. 'Would you like to look around the place a little? See what Ben meant to do to improve the ranch?'

I was surprised by the offer, but accepted. 'I would. I probably already know most of it. You can't imagine how many nights we lay in our bunks, me and Ben, and he talked about his dreams. And about you, Nina.'

That seemed to improve her mood a little, to let her know how much she had meant to Ben. We wandered about the small homestead with the lazy yellow hound ambling after us, me taking in the layout, Nina seemingly lost in memories. Bobby had finished dressing the rabbits and he watched us with sullen eyes.

'There's a second well there, behind the barn,' Nina told me, 'but it needs cleaning out. If you look up ahead, you can see the fold in the hills. Ben was going to build a spreader dam up there to keep water flowing to the flats so we could expand the hayfield.' She stopped, her arms folded beneath her breasts and looked skyward and then back toward the house. 'We wanted to bring some sawn lumber out from Billings, maybe as soon as next spring if we had a good calving year, and start constructing a real house.

'Have you ever been in a soddy when it rains, Ryan?'

'Yes, I have.'

'Mud dripping from the roof. You can't keep a thing clean. It's just impossible.'

'I know.'

She sighed, wiped a strand of her honey-colored hair from her eyes and shrugged. 'Well, we all have our disappointments, don't we?'

'We do.'

'Life is just a series of problems solving.'

'So it seems,' I agreed. Her cheeks were a little flushed with the coolness and her green eyes looked brighter. I thought she would solve this too, get along with her life even if it wasn't what she had been planning for.

'I guess we can't live on expectations,' she said. She had been looking beyond me. Now her eyes met mine directly. 'I do thank you for bringing us that money.'

'Don't mention it.' I found myself holding her gaze longer, feeling an elusive emotion begin to grow somewhere at the bottom of my spine. I shook off the mood, whatever it was.

'Will you be staying in the area?' Nina asked.

'No.' I shook my head. 'I'm on my way to Oregon.'

'With winter setting in!'

'Well – when the weather allows it. I'll probably start making my way south some. I'll probably find some place to hole up until spring.'

'I see,' she said thoughtfully. 'Why couldn't you

115

just "hole up" in Billings, Ryan?'

I couldn't tell her that, of course. I answered evasively, 'I just need to keep moving, Nina.'

'Just a saddle tramp, huh?' she asked with a pursed smile.

'I guess, yes.' I smiled but the words had touched me wrong. Was that all I really was or would ever be? I wondered. I had been headed for Oregon for two years now. Was it just a goal I had placed in my mind because I had no other goal, no real goal?

'Would you like to look at the cattle?' Nina asked. 'Maybe you could give me an idea what I should ask for them. Ben always took care of the selling, you know. I don't know what they're worth. Not much, I suppose,' she said with a small, appealing frown.

'I'd like to, but I don't have the time, really,' I said. I looked to the skies. 'It'll be getting dark before long, and if it snows I want to be under shelter somewhere.'

'Of course,' she said, and we started walking slowly back toward the house. The yellow dog veered this way and that snuffling his way along the ground, looking for scents to interest him. 'Ryan,' Nina said, pausing near the barren elm tree. Her words were hesitant as she said, 'You could spend the night here, you know. In the barn, of course,' she added hastily. 'I mean – that would give you time to rest your horse a little and you could start early in the morning. To – well, wherever it is that you're going.'

I mulled that over. It wasn't a bad idea, although there were obvious complications. 'What would Bobby think about that?' I had to ask.

'It doesn't matter much what Bobby thinks, Ryan,' she said, her voice a little heated. 'This is my home and he's still a kid.'

'Not in his own mind.'

'He's just fourteen. He's not running my life.'

I considered the offer from all sides. Finally I agreed. The black could use a night's rest and so could I. I'd take her up on the offer and stay well out of her way – and Bobby's.

'Thank you. I accept.'

'There's not much hay in the rick,' Nina said, 'and we need what we have,' she added apologetically. 'But there's plenty to be had if you're handy with a scythe.' She nodded toward the field beyond the barn where some poor hay lingered uncut.

'That sounds fair to me,' I agreed cheerfully. 'I'll cut what I can this afternoon and stack it in the barn.'

'Fine. Don't give the cows any. That's Bobby's job. Although,' she said pensively, 'I doubt he remembered it this morning.'

'All right. I'll just lead my horse over and get him settled in, then I'll see what kind of farmer I'd make.'

She laughed almost breathlessly. 'Ryan, I really wanted you to accept the invitation. I haven't had a soul to talk to for a long time except Bobby, and he's just a kid and our conversation just turns to bickering anyway. Now I'll let you get to work. I'm

going to go back to the house and see about starting rabbit stew for dinner.'

She walked away then, and to me it seemed she
was more erect, her carriage more graceful. I had
a smile on my face for a long minute before I even
noticed I was wearing it. I shook my head and put
my thoughts elsewhere as I went to fetch my
horse.

The rest of the afternoon I spent mowing hay.
There was a fair stand of alfalfa, but it had withered and been invaded by wild oats and buffalo
grass. No matter, it was good enough fodder for
the horses and I cut and stacked steadily, my warming body perspiring under my clothes even though
the wind was cool. The sky to the north held clear
until just before sundown when Nina appeared on
the steps of the house and waved her arm,
summoning me to supper.

I washed at the well the best I could and went
into the house which was now warm and scented
with spices and boiling meat and potatoes. Bobby
sat brooding in the corner. At least he had hung
his shotgun up on its wall pegs.

Nina looked fine, her cheeks touched with roses
painted there by the woodfire.

'Better sit down,' she said to me. 'It's just about
ready. Bobby?'

'I ain't hungry.'

'You have to eat.'

'I said I ain't hungry,' the boy said, and he
lurched from his chair to cross to his shotgun. I
kept an eye on him, but he didn't even give me a

backward glance as he stalked angrily from the house, leaving the door open to the cool of the night. Nina stared out at the evening darkness, her hands on her hips, then closed the door and returned to the pot on the stove, ladling out two bowls of rabbit stew for us.

'I'm sorry to be making trouble,' I said, as she smoothed her skirt under her and sat down facing me.

'He'll get over it. I told him you were riding out tomorrow.' I thought there was a touch of regret in her voice, and I had a few of my own even though I knew the situation was impossible.

'Are you still going to move into town?' I asked, as I carefully tasted the hot, spicy stew.

'There's no choice. The two of us can't handle the farm, I know that.'

'Maybe it will work out for the best.'

'Maybe.' She smiled but there was lingering doubt in those deep-green eyes. 'You'll be continuing on to Oregon, I suppose.'

'That's always been my plan,' I replied. We ate in uneasy silence. I was attracted to Nina and she knew it. But there could not be anything between us, not with her problems – and my own. 'Is there any place I could write you?' she asked, holding her spoon just at her lips.

I shook my head. 'I don't know where I'll be.'

'No? Well, it's been nice meeting you, Ryan,' she said.

'It has,' I agreed. Hesitantly I said, 'Maybe I could write to you sometime. If you don't mind.'

119

'I don't.'

'Fine. I'm not much at writing, but maybe you can give me the name of that shop you'll be working at, then well . . .'

'I could do that. How's the stew?'

After that we exchanged only a few words. What was there to say? I would never see her again. I had done my duty and now I was riding on again. Going somewhere. Just somewhere, not knowing what it was I wanted. Or maybe I did, but I could never have it, and so that was the same thing.

After supper Nina dug up an extra blanket for me and I made my way to the barn with the aid of a kerosene lantern which I hung on a nail on the wall while I made up my bed on a pile of straw. Then, turning out the lantern, I rolled up in my blankets and lay awake for a long while, hands behind my head, staring at a single star that I could see glowing brightly beyond the world in a gap between the barn doors.

Morning came slowly. I rose stiff and foggy-headed. Rolling my blankets I went to my horse, rubbed him down and forked some fresh hay into his feed bin.

Then, not yet fully awake I crossed to the barn doors and opened them. I blinked into the morning sunlight and then froze. There were three riders coming in, approaching from the west. I sensed trouble, but there wasn't time to saddle up and run. I wasn't about to start a fight near Nina's house, so there wasn't a thing to do but stand and watch as they approached the ranch.

The one in front I recognized instantly from the horse he rode. It was Bobby Comfrey. I saw sunlight glitter off the star the second rider wore on his coat. I didn't know him, but he looked like trouble. When I could make out the third man's face I knew it was trouble. Of the worst kind.

It was Marshal Coombs from New Madrid, and he was riding grim, a Winchester across his saddle bow, face set darkly. I didn't move. There was no point in it.

When they entered the yard I could see triumph on Bobby's young face, determination in the expressions of the two lawmen. I stepped out into the yard. I had unbuckled Ben Comfrey's gun and let the belt drop to the ground. I didn't raise my hands, however, and they seemed to take offense at that.

'Don't give us any trouble, Ryan!' Coombs commanded me.

'I don't intend to,' I said honestly. Bobby had swung from his horse and ran into the house without hitching his pony.

'This is Sheriff Gallagher of Billings,' Coombs told me. I only nodded. I didn't think shaking hands was appropriate. Bobby had rushed excitedly back out on to the porch and Nina appeared, a shawl across her shoulders, her golden hair still unpinned.

'I told you he was a killer, Sis! I told you what he

was. I knew it.'

'What is this?' Nina asked coolly. Her voice was uninflected, but I could see terror in her eyes.

'This is a wanted man, ma'am,' Gallagher told her. He was small, round and clean shaven. His manner was smug. 'Armed robbery and murder are the charges.'

'I don't believe you,' Nina said, but Gallagher unfolded a Wanted poster with my description on it and handed it down to Bobby who ran to take it eagerly, returning to show it to his sister. Nina scanned the poster and then lowered it mechanically, studying me with obvious sadness. Without another word, she turned and went back into the house, closing the door silently behind her.

'There's a reward, Sis!' Bobby yelled at the closing door. 'Five hundred dollars! And it's ours, isn't it, Sheriff?' The sheriff nodded solemnly, keeping his dark eyes on mine. There was no answer from the house. The morning was silent for a minute with the only sound the wind stirring the high thin branches of the barren elm. Marshal Coombs swung down and walked to me, holding his Colt revolver cocked and ready, his eyes as gloomy and purposeful as ever.

'Let's get your horse, Ryan. We're going to take a little ride.'

In the barn, Coombs had me back to the far corner of the building while he checked my saddle-bags for any hidden gun I might have had. Then he jacked all the cartridges from my

Winchester and jammed it into its scabbard. He nodded to me to saddle up the black which I did under the watchful eyes of both lawmen.

'Would it do any good to explain everything?' I asked.

'It might if I was a judge,' Coombs said almost sorrowfully. 'Tell me – did you have to shoot Jarvis down?'

'I had to.'

'I thought so. I knew they were lying to me. When I followed along out to Art Lennox's place I found the three of them. Art's arm was fractured. Veronica was giving him hell for not shooting you. Henry Jarvis was dead, of course. He still had his six-gun in his hand.'

'They wanted to gun me down.'

'Jarvis is no loss to the world. It's a good thing you didn't shoot the woman. They damn sure would have hanged you for that,' Coombs said, as I finished cinching my saddle and slipped the bit into the black horse's mouth.

'You almost seem to believe me, Marshal,' I said, as I swung aboard.

'Doesn't matter,' he replied. 'There's a few other dead men behind you, Ryan. Alton McCallister won't let go of those charges, and he won't forget you robbing him on his own train. No, I'm pretty sure there's a reason for a lot of what you did. It doesn't matter. They'll probably hang you anyway.'

That seemed like a reasonable assessment of my situation. I had no one to vouch for me. My only witness to the shoot-out at Yellow Tongue had been Ben Comfrey, and he would bear witness no more. In fact I was suspected of killing him as well. As we rode slowly from the yard of the rundown little farm, the two lawmen flanked me at a careful distance so that I could not grab for either of them which would have been a desperate and suicidal move on my part. I turned my head back and saw Bobby Comfrey standing on the porch, arms crossed, watching us as we departed. His arms were folded; there was a satisfied smile on his face. I saw no sign of Nina. Was she crying now, cursing, indifferent, having expected nothing more from the unforgiving universe than one more disappointment?

We rode on across the snowy land toward Billings.

The two lawmen had a conversation about what they were going to do with me. Did the county sheriff have custody, or the town marshal of New Madrid? I had been captured in the county, of course, but the warrants were out of New Madrid. Marshal Coombs reminded Gallagher that it was Alton McCallister who wanted me back in New Madrid for the trial, and that seemed to settle the question. McCallister's railroad was the word of law in these distant settlements. His was the power of influence and the promise of future prosperity. Without the railroad, as both men knew, their communities, bypassed or snubbed by the Colorado Northern, could suffer the fate of hundreds of other now withering hamlets on the plains.

We reached Billings in early afternoon and I was temporarily placed in a cell occupied by a sleeping drunk with a battered and bruised face. I stretched out on a wooden bunk hung from the stone walls on two iron chains while the sheriff and Marshal Coombs completed their paperwork.

Coombs approached me as the high barred window in the cell was growing dark and told me that he was waiting for morning to return me to New Madrid.

'I don't favor riding out into the night with you. It's cold and I'm hungry. I'm going to the restaurant and then take a room at the hotel.' He appeared almost lugubrious. His pouched eyes reflected sadness, but it was only the weariness of life they showed and not pity for me. 'I'll see that you're fed.'

'My horse. . . ?'

'He'll be attended to,' Coombs promised. Then Gallagher handed me a thin blanket through the bars of the cell and, after waiting around for a lean, expressionless deputy to come and watch the jail, the two officers of the law tramped out into the rapidly falling dusk to dine.

I lay back wrapped tightly in my blanket, staring at the gray stone ceiling. I thought of escape, of course – I had read a few of those dime novels where the hero forms a cunning plan of escape, or some friend tosses him a gun through the jail-house window – but I had less cunning than those heroes of fiction. And I had not a friend in the

world. I closed my eyes and slept. At seven or so
the deputy awakened me and I ate from a tin tray
– grits and ham. Then I went back to sleep immediately and dreamed of Oregon.

And, off and on, of Nina.

NINE

Come dawn I was shaken from my cot and taken out into the office. The morning was chill and it was dark inside the jailhouse despite the low burning lanterns. Marshal Coombs looked as weary and sad as he had the day before. It seemed he was just another man slogging through his last days at a job with limited rewards. The marshal and Gallagher seated me on a wooden chair and fitted me with a pair of manacles.

'Sorry, Ryan,' Coombs said, 'but New Madrid's a long way and I'll be alone with you. You have shown a tendency for violence.'

I didn't answer. They snapped the locks shut on the cuffs – at least I was allowed to wear them in front, since riding a horse otherwise was impossible. Still the cold steel chafed almost immediately and I realized fully that there was no way to slip them. This was it. My next stop would be the jail in New Madrid. Then, soon after, I would mount a scaffold with Alton McCallister watching me with cool disdain. He would feel nothing but smug satisfaction as they placed a hangman's rope around my throat and adjusted the knot to the side so that it would crack my neck cleanly. He was not the sort of man to feel guilt, no matter that every bit of this was caused by his own unrelenting greed and need for power.

'Let's go,' Coombs said, and I got to my feet. They placed my hat on my head and we marched out into the orange-gray of early dawn. The streets were deserted, the rime thick underfoot. At the stable our horses were saddled and ready. I swung awkwardly into the saddle, resting my hand on the pommel. Coombs mounted his own stocky bay and nodded to the stable hand who handed me the reins to my black, and then together we rode out on to the cold street where here and there we saw shopkeepers starting to open up for another work-day.

Coombs was in no rush; there was no sense in hurrying. Reaching the outskirts of town we settled into a plodding pace. The horses blew steam from their nostrils. Behind us their tracks were deep and well defined in the snow. The skies held clear as we rode without speaking for mile after long mile. I didn't mind the silence. It gave me time for long reflection on my aimless life.

I had left home early, intent on making my fortune in the vast West. Everyone knew there were fortunes to be made. There was gold, silver, open land free for the taking, buffalo and beaver. I never made my fortune; the West was too big for me, it seemed.

Then against all odds I found a woman I might have cared for, who might have cared for me. But now Nina was lost to me as well. What did she think, I wondered? Had this been enough to convince her I was a murderer, had perhaps indeed killed Ben as Bobby had insisted? Maybe so; who knew?

I would never see her again anyway, so it did not matter.

'There's a creek up ahead,' Coombs said, pointing toward a long stand of cottonwood trees and willow, all now gray and barren. Their pattern indicated that they were lined along a water source. The trees were maybe a mile off. 'We'll pull up there for a while. My butt can only take so many hours in the saddle anymore.'

'Sorry I had to trouble you to make the ride,' I said with a grin.

'I am, too,' he sighed. 'When I was younger, Ryan . . . hell, down in New Mexico I tracked a renegade white man for three days. And that was across desert in August . . . well,' he added, his voice trailing off, 'that was a long time ago.'

'Did you catch him?' I asked the lawman. 'The renegade?'

Coombs looked sideways at me from under those bushy eyebrows. 'Caught him and hanged him.'

I nodded and we fell into silence. After a few more minutes had passed beneath our horses' hoofs, I said, 'It can't be much fun – a man your age – having to hit the trail. Not in this kind of weather anyway.'

Coombs continued to eye me as if my words had a secret meaning. He shrugged heavily at length and answered, 'It never was no fun. As to having to do it now, no, Ryan: it's no fun at all. I kind of resent the people who make me have to get out of my warm little jailhouse and go hunting for them.

'But,' he continued more wistfully, 'what else could I do anyway? They don't pay lawmen nothin', so you can't save nothing. I can't afford a parcel of land and I don't know if I have the ambition to start all over again.'

Again a silence descended on us. The snow wasn't deep, but the wind had increased, making it uncomfortable. There was no timber to break the blowing wind. I saw only here and there a gray, spindly stand of willows or dead cottonwoods and here and there a big old lonesome oak standing on some small hummock, seeming to survey the empty, noiseless plains.

'We cut off here,' Coombs said, and I saw we had neared the stream he had indicated earlier. I nodded and we started down a sandy trail. Deer and elk had used it, breaking up the snow. Ahead I could see the coldly glistening silver of the creek through the iron-gray trunks of the thin trees.

We pulled up as we reached it. It was wider than I had thought, maybe fifty feet or so across to the far side. Here and there were ice-fringes where the sun could not reach the shadowy coldness. The murmuring sounds the water made in passing were pleasant, almost melodic.

It wasn't enough to make me forget that this man, like him or not, was the one taking me back to be hanged in New Madrid – for I had no doubt that Alton McCallister would see that I did hang even if he had to bribe the judge and every possible juror.

I swung down and stretched my back. I placed my hat on my saddlehorn and listened to the wind and the river. Holding my manacled hands before me I waited for Marshal Coombs's orders. He looked up and downstream as if expecting an ambush. I figured it was a habit left over from the days when wild Indians were plentiful in these parts. He turned toward me.

'You go ahead, Ryan,' he instructed. 'Just bob your head and drink like a bird.'

'I can't do much else,' I said with a grin, gesturing with my manacled hands.

He stood away from me and watched, his rifle in his hand as I knelt and bowed my head to the creek, sipping at the icy water.

'It's fresh and sweet as it could be,' I said sitting back on my heels. 'Now if you happen to have a sausage and a loaf of bread, we could have a little picnic while the horses have their fill.'

Coombs's mouth approached a smile. 'Don't talk to me about food just now. I missed my breakfast this morning – and I'm going to miss my lunch.'

'Sorry,' I said, rising awkwardly. I waited for more instructions.

'Now get back by your horse while I drink.'

I nodded and retreated to where the black

stood, impatiently waiting for his turn to drink. Except I didn't go back quite as far as the marshal believed. And as he took his tin cup and bent to the creek, I moved forward even more. I eased up on him silently, just hoping his head wouldn't turn. But something on the far bank had caught Coombs's eyes and he rested on his knees, looking at it for just a few seconds too long, and when I figured I was close enough to make my move, I tried it.

There was no choice about it. I didn't relish the idea of hemp tightening around my neck. I leaped to him and shoved my boot against the small of his back. Hard, with all the strength I had. Coombs had seen me at the last second. His startled eyes lifted to me and he tried to grab for his Winchester, but he was too slow. He yelled something that might have been a curse and plunged face forward into the racing icy water of the creek.

My last glimpse of him was when he had reached nearly mid-stream and he came up coughing and choking, his hair plastered down on his skull. He shook his fist at me violently as the current swept him away.

I didn't wait around. Coombs might run up against a snag or a rock and get himself out of the water faster than I thought he could, sodden clothing and all. I mounted the black, grabbed the reins to the marshal's horse and rode away from the river without glancing back.

Half a mile away I halted the black and swung down. I went to the marshal's saddle-bags and searched for the key to the handcuffs I was wearing. I had no luck. He must have kept the key in one of his pockets. That left me with yet another problem. I took the marshal's canteen and a few small items from his saddlags – a stub of a pencil, a box of spare ammo and some woolen socks.

That left me with the question of what to do with Coombs' horse. I fully intended to return to New Madrid, but not as a prisoner. I still had business to settle with the railroad.

But for now I needed somehow to slip back into Billings. If I timed it right and arrived in darkness I thought I could get away with it. Not many people there knew my face, nor did anyone but the sheriff know my horse, and he certainly wasn't expecting me back there. The stocky bay that Coombs rode was a different matter; it could be known to any number of people in Billings. Clumsily, with my manacled hands I uncinched Coombs's saddle, letting it fall to the ground. I slipped the bay's bit and slapped it on the flank. It took off, startled, and ran for a hundred feet or so. Then it stopped, looking back at me with offended eyes.

Unless the horse doubled back toward the river, and it seemed more likely it would just continue on home to New Madrid, Coombs would never find it on this day. If he did, his butt would be a lot sorer than ever riding it bareback to his office without even reins to guide the horse.

I didn't have time to worry about things like that. The marshal had treated me right, but I knew he would shoot me if it came to the point where he thought it was necessary to do so. I nudged my horse's flanks with my boot-heels and started quickly on my way, doubling back toward Billings.

The first thing, of course was to get the irons off my wrists. I thought there was one person I could trust to help me.

The sun was riding low in a cloudless purple sky when I came to the outskirts of Billings, but it was still not dark enough for my purposes. I remembered a shallow pond just on the outskirts where dense willows grew and I could hide my horse and myself and I started in that direction, watching as early lamps began to flicker on across the town.

Finding myself in among the heavy willow brush I swung down and tried to plan my moves. It would take a deal of caution and a lot of risk to accomplish what I had in mind. I was squatting down, my hat tilted back on my head when I felt eyes on me and saw a shadowed figure nearer the pond. I whirled and almost drew my gun before I saw it was a kid with a fishing pole. Maybe one of the ones I had met the other day, I couldn't be sure. He stood there in the lengthening shadows, his frayed straw hat casting a long shadow across his face.

The kid was eight years old or so, and something about him made him look a little dull-witted. His mouth was turned down heavily. His forehead seemed unnaturally knobby.

'Hello,' I said. He took a cautious step toward me.

'What are you doing here?' he asked, still frowning.

'Why, I'm just waiting for my friend. I'm going to play a trick on him.'

'What friend?' he asked uncertainly. He didn't appear to be frightened, just curious. I held my hands beneath my coat and he hadn't noticed the handcuffs. I decided to try something risky. The man I needed to see had tools and I thought could be trusted. Why not send a message rather than trying to slip into town unseen?

'My friend is a man named Pez. Do you know him?'

The kid shook his head. His mouth hung open loosely.

'The man with the beard who works at the hotel. You might have seen him up on the roof patching it up.'

His eyes brightened. 'I know him! He lives in the tool shed behind the kitchen. Sometimes he gives me bent nails.'

'Does he? Well, he's my friend. I want you to take something to him.'

I fished awkwardly in my pockets, turning away from the kid. First I handed him a dime which caused his eyes to brighten even more. 'This is for you if you do what I'm asking, all right? If you don't, I'll have to come and take it away from you.' His head nodded vigorously and he studied the dime in pleased amazement.

'Can you read, boy?' I asked.

'No, sir. I haven't managed that yet,' he said

135

doubtfully, apparently fearing that he might lose the dime.

Glad of that, I hastily scribbled a note to Pez, using my saddle as a desk top. '*Pez, I'm cuffed. Bring tools to the pond back of town. Ryan.*' Folding it, I gave it to the boy and warned him, 'Don't stop to buy any penny candies or anything, before you find Pez.'

He promised he wouldn't and I watched as he dashed off, weaving his way agilely through the willow brush. I wondered if I hadn't made a mistake, but then again, most kids are more trustworthy than adults. No matter, there had been no other choice. I settled in to wait.

The dying sun made the pond a violet mirror. Somewhere I heard a coyote bark and an anxious farm dog barked back angrily, warning the wild creature. It was growing colder by the minute, the sky losing all of its color except for a long crimson pennant hanging limply above the western horizon.

I heard someone approaching and I yanked my Winchester from its scabbard and slid deeper back into the shadows. A low whistle sounded from twenty or thirty feet away. I whistled back, hoping that it was Pez, hoping he was alone. It was. In a few minutes the lanky, gray-bearded trapper emerged into the clearing where my horse stood and looked around with narrowed eyes.

'I'm over here, Pez,' I said, stepping out of the heavy shadows.

'What kind of scrape have you gotten yourself

into, Ryan?' he asked with a tolerant smile. His eyes took in the manacles at a glance.

'Some old trouble caught up with me. I'll tell you sometime. For now' – I held out my hands – 'can you get these off?'

'Sure.' He was carrying a canvas bag with tools borrowed from the tool shed at the hotel, and a lantern. I walked to him as total darkness began to settle. Pez told me, 'I'm going to have to have some light. Them willows should shield it from anyone in town. Anyone does happen to spot it, it won't look no brighter than a firefly.'

Squatting he struck a match and lit the wick to the oil lamp. The wick was turned down so low that barely a fizzle of light could be seen. I had to move close to it so that Pez could work. From his bag he withdrew a hammer and chisel.

'Roll that rock over here,' he instructed me, nodding toward a head-sized piece of granite near my feet. 'I'll strike the chain first. That way if anyone does come up on us, you'll at least have use of your hands.'

I nodded and moved the rock nearer to the lantern. Pez crouched. Glancing up at me and then down at the chain placed across the rock, he positioned the chisel and struck down with the hammer. The ring as it struck seemed ominously loud, but the chisel cleaved the chain neatly with one stroke.

'Keep an eye out now,' Pez said. He had taken a hacksaw from the bag and now, intent and know-ledgeable, he went to work at the cuffs themselves.

It seemed a long time, but in only minutes Pez had freed my wrists from the cuffs. I rubbed my chafed wrists and thanked him.

'It's nothin', Ryan. If it wasn't for you I'd likely have starved or frozen this winter. I really would like to hear your story – but not here and now. Next time we meet.'

'Next time we meet,' I promised, shaking his hand warmly. He nodded, smiled, and turned to toss the handcuffs out into the pond where they sank out of sight with a small plunk no louder than a fish breaking the surface.

'Good luck to you, son,' he said, and then with his lantern extinguished again and his canvas bag in his hand, he too disappeared into the night and the woods, leaving me alone. I wasted no time climbing back aboard the black and circling away from the town. Who knew – the kid might have said something about the strange man giving him a dime. I hoped I had caused Pez no trouble.

On my own again I headed out on to the prairie. Now I could just glimpse the rising rim of the moon cresting the western horizon to begin its lonely skyward climb. There was a faint sheen of moonlight glimmering on the snowy ground, enough for me to avoid prairie dog holes and other obstacles.

I felt like a free man again, but I wasn't free in any sense. I was wanted by the law and needed to get south, away from Montana and my troubles. But I wasn't ready to go just yet. I couldn't leave just yet. There was still unfinished business to be attended to. I guided my black horse westward once more. Once again riding to where no sane man would wish to go.

Where I was honor bound to ride.

TEN

The great iron horse rested a quarter of a mile from the trestle spanning the maw of Yellow Tongue Gorge. By the moonlight I could see its great powering wheels and the diamond stack rising above the barrel of its mammoth fire-breathing chest. Now the iron horse stood inert, still, awaiting the prompting of the engineer's whip to roar to life and thunder its way westward toward Pocatello and other points west, south and north as the railroad's silvery web of rails joined together distant towns and outposts.

On the far side of the gorge I could see that the rails the train would follow into Idaho had already been joined with the western tongue of the trestle. They had done it. The train – in the public imagination – would roll on, a great stride toward the building of the West. It would be welcomed, cheered. Praised by front-page editorials in the newspapers. The railroad itself would be honored and applauded as a benefactor, a bringer of a lifeline to the struggling communities.

No matter that this train was a cheat, a destroyer of men, a death train. Would any of the lumberjacks, engineers, surveyors and laborers who had brought the train this far ever be paid? I doubted it. How many of those left behind by it would be willing to trail after it, let alone attempt to take the mighty Colorado Northern to court for their money? They had no chance, I knew. The railroad would laugh at them as it had laughed at me. And if they fought too hard they would be killed, as Ben Comfrey had been killed. As they had tried to kill me.

The stars were bright in a cold sky despite the sullen half moon among them. The trestle was a huge black timberweb across the dark chasm of the Yellow Tongue Gorge. Something about it humbled me even as I shook with anger. Men had made something larger than themselves and that was always admirable, remarkable really. I had had a small part in it. I wished the killing urge were not on me.

Because I planned to kill this magnificent creation.

I knew the railroad camp as well as anyone; the darkness of the night didn't bother me. I set off on foot, hearing the sound of a man cursing, the chorus of music from another bunkhouse. A door slammed. The camp was alive with men, but no one was standing guard on this cold night in this isolated country.

I made my way to the storeroom without being seen and breached the flimsy hasp on the door easily. I did not light a match. Starlight shone feebly through the single high window in the shed, but I searched mostly by touch. Knowing where the coal oil was kept, I eased that way, my finger searching the shelves where I knew there would be a can that I could fill from the fifty-gallon drums.

Someone passed outside – two men talking in low voices. I could not catch the words. I crouched down and let them pass. When they were gone I began again. My fingers slid over various objects until they touched the smooth curved steel of a coal oil can. I hefted it and found that it was nearly full. Good, that saved me one step. I unscrewed the cap and sniffed it to reassure myself and then started out again. I found myself smiling as I reached the door, slid out into the night and made my silent way back across the railroad camp. For a man who abhors destruction of any kind normally, I was enjoying myself vastly.

'It won't be long now, Ben,' I whispered. 'They should have paid us.' Instead of treating us like dogs, shooting Ben Comfrey dead in the snow.

I recrossed the railroad tracks and walked a hundred yards south. I knew where the timber trail was. I had crossed over it and back twice a day for two months. Even in the night I had no trouble finding the head of the trail which led down into the gorge and back up to the timber slope on the far side. Except on this night I wasn't going to climb up on that side again. My work lay at the very bottom of the chasm, where the trestle pilings sunk their heads into the solid earth beside the rapidly flowing Yellow Tongue River.

Nothing moved. There was not a single sound in the world as I started down the narrow trail. It was so utterly still that when a distant owl hooted, I started. I wondered if there were guards down here in the cool depths, or above me on the trestle with their rifles trained on me. It seemed extremely doubtful. What would they be guarding against? Besides, I was so deeply lost in shadow now that no one above could see me unless I lit a lamp or struck a match.

Which was exactly what I intended to do – but not just yet.

The river snaked past, dark and swift. The eons of following its course were what had carved the gorge out of primal stone. The river would flow on, long after any man-made structure had rotted and fallen away.

I nearly walked into one of the massive pilings, so dark was it in the bowels of the gorge. I felt the thick timber and paced carefully ahead, finding its mate. I looked up at the complicated bracing of the trestle overhead.

These two, I decided, would do it.

Crouching, I opened the coal oil can, tossing the lid away – there wouldn't be another use for that. I began splashing the coal oil on the spars, drenching them, first one then the other. What was left I spread in pools around their bases. I looked up once more at the huge dark web of timbers above me, nodded to myself and lit a match. The first match extinguished itself in the puddle of oil. I tried a second and it fizzled as it hit the ground, then sparked, then brightened and flared. As I backed away I watched as yellow-bright flames began to lick their way up along the piling. Then the puddled coal oil at its base blossomed into a hot rose and simultaneously the second piling caught.

One low cross-beam had already begun to smoke and within moments the dry new timber was burning hotly. The flames lighted the adjacent stone wall of the gorge with weird red light and the dark smoke began to rise like an evil ghost weaving its way through the intricate structure overhead, climbing toward the sky.

I got out of there as fast as I could.

I made for the foot of the trail, glancing back once across my shoulder to see that the flames were climbing higher and higher, spreading flame and heat traversely along the bracing timbers as they devoured lumber and creosote. The night was ablaze and I was caught in the glare of my own deed. I could hear distant shouts now and I raced on up the trail, falling once to bang my knee painfully on a rock.

Cresting the head of the trail I could see tiny figures racing toward me from the camp. I raced toward the safety of surrounding shadows, leaving the hot glare of my crime behind me. By the time the first man had reached the head of the trail I was deep in the shadows of the pine woods. Bending over I breathed deeply, filling my aching lungs with huge gulps of cold air.

Men from all across the camp in all stages of dress were rushing toward the trestle. Why, I couldn't say. It was obvious that there was nothing anyone could do to save the structure now. Flames had reached as far as the timbers supporting the rails themselves. Great leaping red and yellow spirals of flame sheeting the night sky. Smoke stretched up to the stars, shutting out their silver light. I had done that, but I had no pride in it. It was the work of many months by many men, and that part of it I regretted. That was all that I regretted. I did not regret the harm I had done to the railroad.

I started on through the smoky darkness, having no fear of being seen or halted. There were so many men running around in confusion that no one had time to give me a second glance.

I was arrogant with overconfidence. And out of luck. Making my way back toward the camp again I walked almost directly into one of the many men who could recognize me in those conditions. It was Tom, one of Alton McCallister's bodyguards. It was the third time we had met and I saw his head turn. Our eyes met and he strode toward me. Tom was wearing a buffalo coat and a black slouch hat. His hand held a rifle. I stopped and stood still to meet him as the flames rose higher into the night sky. For a moment he paused, unsure of himself as I marched directly toward him, my hand raised as if in greeting.

Then Tom was sure and he shouted, a cry unheard above the general uproar. I didn't wait to see what he would do next, I lowered my head and charged into him and we hit the ground, Tom's rifle flying free as I chopped a short right into his jaw.

Tom grunted, tried to knee me and then wriggled free enough to unleash a barrage of short blows at my head. He was on his back and, without leverage, his blows had little effect. A sharp left did land solidly on my ear and set bells to ringing in my skull, but I had better position and better leverage. I threw a fisted right hand into his neck and followed with another that landed solidly on his temple.

Tom's eyes rolled back and he lay still. I rose panting from the dark earth, flung his rifle away into the woods and started on my way again, my legs a little wobbly from the brief exchange. Everyone was rushing in the opposite direction, away from the camp and the locomotive. There was an eerie glow across the railroad camp, the earth was red and the fronts of the log buildings appeared black through the drifting smoke.

I reached the locomotive in minutes and mounted the iron steps to the cab. The engineer was there wearing regular street clothes. He had apparently rushed down to the locomotive to stand ready for orders. He started to shout at me, but I showed him my pistol. He backed toward the coal tender, his hands raised, eyes wide.

'What are you doing?' he asked in a trembling voice.

'Fire this thing up,' I ordered.

'I can't . . .'

'You'd better!' I said, cocking my pistol. 'If anybody asks you, tell them the boss wants the train backed away from the trestle, just in case.'

He decided against arguing with me and set to work, starting a blaze in the firebox. While we waited for a head of steam to build up, I ordered him to step down to the ground with me. He looked around excitedly, hoping for help, looking for somewhere to run. I nudged him with my pistol.

'Uncouple the Pullmans. I just want the locomotive.'

'We can't back up if we do that,' he said with terror-stricken eyes.

'We're not going back,' I told him. 'We're going ahead.'

'We can't. . . .'

'Yes, we can. Who knows, maybe the trestle will hold. Unless you just want it here and now,' I said, gesturing again with my revolver.

He didn't like that any better and within seconds he had uncoupled the cars from the locomotive. No one was paying any attention to us as far as I could see. The trestle was a quarter of a mile ahead and everyone's eyes were on the raging flames. Still, you never knew. I kept searching the surrounding night with my eyes, expecting anything.

'Now what?' the engineer asked.

'Now we're going to take a ride. Just you and me.'

'Listen, mister, I got a wife and kids—'

'Get this locomotive rolling!' I hissed. We climbed back up into the cab and the engineer stood staring at the pressure gauge. He was delaying and I knew it. 'That's enough steam to get it moving, isn't it?'

'Normally I need—'

'Quit stalling. That's enough steam, get us rolling!'

I thought he was going to continue arguing, but probably he could see that there was no point in it. Yanking back on the heavy gear lever and levering down the huge iron braking bar I saw him swallow a bitter curse as we felt the first jerky movement of the drive wheels.

'Open it up, Engineer. I'm in a hurry to reach my destination.'

'Hell's where you're bound!' he shouted back frantically.

'Likely,' I agreed.

The train started slowly to pick up speed. Far away I saw someone turn and point at the locomotive as smoke rose from its stack to mingle with the smoke of the fiery night. No one else seemed to notice that the train was moving, driving relentlessly toward the flaming trestle over Yellow Tongue Gorge.

'Open the throttle wide, Engineer!' I yelled. 'Then jump.'

'I can't jump!' he screamed back.

'You can. You've got a wife and kids, you say: if you want to see them again, jump now before it's too late.'

He looked once more at me, once at the gun I held and turned and leaped off into space. I saw him land, roll and lie flat on his face against the snow-patched earth. I didn't wait any longer myself. I leaped from the opposite side of the cab, landing roughly on the ground. The wheels of the locomotive seemed to thunder past bare inches from my head, but I was clear and up and running in a staggering, lurching jog-trot toward the woods.

Recovering my wits I slowed to a steady walk, holstered my gun and walked on. Turning my head I saw no one pursuing me. All eyes had been on the roaring flames engulfing the trestle. Now as the men became aware of what was going on, their heads turned toward the roaring behemoth bearing down on them, uncontrolled, unstoppable.

The iron horse trundled on relentlessly; eyeless and witless, it surged past the helpless railroad crews and forward on to the flame-engulfed trestle, pawing its way through the flames and curlicues of black smoke, an implacable brute. From the moment the carrier wheels touched the blackened timbers of the trestle and an agonized, splintering sound rose into the dreadful night, it was obvious that the burned-out trestle could never withstand the terrible weight of the onrushing iron behemoth, and as the drive wheels pawed at the fire-shimmering rails, the structure began to crack and wither beneath it.

In moments the entire trestle was buckling and blackened timbers fell, shredded into the depths of the stony gorge. Then the locomotive, striving to rush onward as its designers had intended, lost purchase and it dropped its head and fell in stunned surrender to the rocks below, sending up sparks and shrieks of metal upon stone as a death dirge as men halted in their rush toward the gorge and watched the dying machine destroy the remaining blackened timbers and land far below with a crescendo of shrieking roars which filled the long canyon with echoes of its death. Steam rushed from its ruptured boiler and filled the gorge, white smoke chasing black until the last throb of its engine ceased.

My path was well-lighted. Flames had brightened the sky to the colored brilliance of a fiery sunset. I passed Tom. He was on his hands and knees, shaking his head. He looked up at me, but made no move to impede my passing. There was nothing he could do and we both knew it.

I found my black horse waiting where I had left it. For a change he was not watching me patiently to see what devilry I had planned for him. He was nervous, pulling at his tether. Firelight danced in his dark eyes. I soothed him with my hand, untied him and swung aboard. Then we were away, weaving through the dark pine forest while the sky continued to glow brightly and drifting smoke to obscure the stars.

We were away, riding south. Where we were bound I did not know, but there are times in life when it is more important to get away from a situation rather than to travel to a particular destination. This was one of them.

Come daylight I was still in the saddle. I was weary and the black horse tired of carrying me over wild country. I swung down and let him rest while I tried to cobble some sort of plan together.. Casper, down in Wyoming was the biggest town on my route, but I didn't think we could make it that far the shape we were in. My best hope was to try to find some fair-sized town between here and there, one that at least had a hotel of some kind and lie up there. I still had most of my money with me. With luck and economy, perhaps even enough to tide us over until spring. I might even be able to find some kind of work around town.

I swung aboard the black again and we began our plodding way southward. It was not the direction I would have chosen as free man. But I was not a free man, not yet, and so with each mile I rode farther and farther away from Nina.

I found the town in a driving rainstorm which, if it continued until dark, would become a snow storm. I saw no signs to advise me what it was called; perhaps it had no name. It was only a ramshackle collection of log huts and shacks with two or three sawn-lumber buildings, each as unimpressive as the last, but from the awning of the middle building hung a wind-blown shingle reading 'Hotel' and I decided that the town, such as it was, was close enough to heaven for me.

With the horse put up in a rickety stable, I registered at the hotel desk. I asked the man what the name of the town was, and he told me, Skogie, and waited for me to laugh. I didn't even smile. I thought it was a fine town, Skogie, with a fine dry hotel and a fine mattress on which I rested my weary head and slept for a long, long time.

I rose to find by the dawn's light a new fall of snow, maybe eighteen inches of it. I looked out my window at it for a long time, pleased with myself. I was going nowhere. I had enough money in my pocket to become a temporary resident of Skogie, enough money to feed myself and keep warm. I might even buy myself a new shirt and a new pair of jeans, a hat – after I had eaten and rested a little more. My plan was to become as indolent as possible for awhile. Let it snow all it wanted to, I couldn't care less!

From time to time those first few days I tried sitting at a desk they had in the shabby lobby of the hotel and composing a letter to Nina in Billings. I got as far as addressing the envelope easily. It was what to write on the blank sheet of paper staring up at me that got me tangled up. I still had no address; I was still on the run and a long way from Oregon. I could never go back to where she was. I just sat at the desk for long minutes, wondering if she had moved into town to live above that hairdresser's shop. I wondered if Bobby had gone with her. I wondered if they had paid him that $500 reward on my head since it was he who had turned me in and Marshal Coombs who had lost me again . . . I wondered how her eyes sparkled in the starlight.

Then I would rise, crumple the never-begun

letter and toss it away. Face it: I was nothing but a saddle tramp, a drifter, no matter what I used to tell myself about Oregon, about somehow buying a piece of land out there, settling down. I was no prize to myself; how could I ever expect a woman like Nina to have serious thoughts about me?

By the second week I was tired of being a layabout. I found a part-time job sweeping up and stocking goods in the general store. The man who hired me, one McCready by name, was holding the job open for his son who was back East studying, but he reckoned his boy wouldn't be traveling with winter having set in.

My life settled into a routine. Mornings I cleaned up at the store for two hours or so then had a leisurely lunch. In the afternoons I worked another two hours. I felt like I was getting lazy and satisfied, but there wasn't much else to do and the work paid my way. As a matter of fact at the end of the month I had more money than I'd had when I rode into Skogie. And I had managed to stay warm and fed! The deprivations of the previous month were just a memory.

Still, I kept an eye on any traveler arriving in town. I never knew which one of them might be a lawman or a bounty hunter with a wanted poster folded in his pocket. Not that there were many new arrivals in Skogie – it wasn't the kind of place people came to if they had better choices. The days went by slowly, evenly. The weather held generally good although the streets of Skogie were deep in muddy goo and slush, and the skies were generally ominous and gray. I minded none of it. No one was looking for me; my life dull as it was, was settled and suited me just fine for the time being. I had at least a nodding acquaintance with most everyone in town and I felt welcome and safe there.

Now and then if the weather was good I'd take the black horse out to exercise him. At times I played a little penny-ante poker or drank a beer with the men. I flirted a little with the waitress and read a book or two. Life wasn't good, but it was trouble-free which can mean something if you'd been in a situation like mine. All in all I hadn't a care in the world and was just waiting lazily for spring to come.

Which was why it was such a shock when I walked into Francee's Golden West Restaurant and saw Alton McCallister occupying a corner table, his eyes locked on to mine.

ELEVEN

There was no doubt at all that the railroad boss recognized me immediately. Maybe someone had told him that I would be in for dinner. His arms were stiff, his hands red and blistered extending from the frayed cuffs of a once fine jacket. His eyes were bleary, his thin red hair uncombed, fringed across his forehead. He looked pale and haggard. The man had done some hard traveling, it seemed. I glanced around but saw no other railroad toughs.

I decided to get it over with and I walked to his table as his eyes glared at me with sheer hatred.

'Hello, McCallister,' I said. The scrape of the wooden chairlegs against the floor seemed loud. I looked around but no one else seemed to be aware of any confrontation among them. 'Looks like you had a long ride.'

'Ryan – I'll curse you until you're dead, and that won't be long. Then I'll curse you over your grave. You ruined me!'

'Oh?' I folded my hands together on the table. I

had tilted back my hat to study McCallister more closely. He was a beaten man, I decided, but that didn't make him less deadly.

'My career is shot,' he said, in a raspy voice unlike his formerly cultured baritone. Maybe the cold weather had had an effect on his throat. He leaned forward more intently. There was a cup of coffee in front of him but he paid no attention to it. 'I had stock options in the Colorado Northern, too. They were contingent on completing the Yellow Tongue spur on schedule.'

'And at the lowest cost possible,' I said mildly.

'Of course! What do you mean?' he asked warily.

'I mean you could have done an honest job of it and paid your workmen, but you got so greedy you had to make a little more and then a little more here and there, no matter that the men who were tearing their tendons and breaking their bones for the railroad weren't getting paid.'

'Oh, that,' he said, flapping a hand as if that were unimportant. 'You don't understand. . . .' he said more hoarsely than ever. 'They *fired* me!'

'That's what I figured,' I answered.

Did he want pity, sympathy – or was he just explaining why he was going to try to kill me?

'My wife and I were building a house in Pocatello. I can't afford to complete it now. No one will ever take me on in the railroad industry again. I'm ruined!'

'Yeah,' I said as coldly as I could, 'it can happen.'

'It wouldn't have happened!' he exploded, and for a minute I thought he was going to go for his pistol. 'If it hadn't been for . . . you.' He was having a hard time speaking. Emotion was making it an effort for him to talk.

'McCallister,' I said quietly, 'you can only push a man so far. I would have thought a man of your experience would have learned that.' I fished in the pocket of my jeans while Alton McCallister watched me suspiciously. I slid a silver dollar from my pocket and placed it on the table in front of him.

'Remember?' I said. 'I owed you a dollar. I'm a man who always pays his debts.'

He stared for a long time at the shiny silver dollar then his eyes returned to mine and they were not normal eyes. They were hateful, animal, and I saw the flicker in them a moment before he made his move.

'So do I always pay my debts,' McCallister said wildly. Then he tried to jump to his feet, draw his holstered gun and kick over the table all at once. He just wasn't good enough: it wasn't his game. He should have stuck to the railroad business.

I hit the floor on my belly, and as McCallister fired two wild shots, one of them punching through the heavy oak table, I braced myself on my elbows and fired up into his body. He staggered back, slammed into the wall and fired again, his bullet gouging the polished wooden floor of the restaurant. He sagged to the floor then, his back smearing the white-painted wall with crimson, and sat there, his gun in his lap, his eyes no longer alive with furies and snakes. I gradually became aware of the shouts, screams and conversation around me.

'Everyone saw it, Ryan. He fired first!' a voice said excitedly.

'Is he dead?' someone asked. 'As dead as he's going to get,' another voice replied.

They were hunched over McCallister. Two townsmen helped me to my feet, asking me if I was OK.

Was I? I didn't know. I turned, picked up my hat and started out of the restaurant, only vaguely aware of the chaos around me. McCallister was dead. It was over – maybe. He was sitting there, an inert corpse with his gun in his cold hand . . . and a shiny silver dollar on the floor beside him.

I didn't like it. I didn't like myself suddenly. Had it all been worth it? I was no longer so sure. I knew one thing: I had to get out of Skogie, go . . . some-where. *Somewhere*, which was where I had always been headed. I didn't want to answer questions; I didn't want to risk the chance that the law might be the one to ask them. I found myself in the stable without remembering how I had gotten there. My head lowered to the horse blanket thrown over the stall's divider. I stood there for a long while, feeling a faint trembling in my body.

Then I straightened up, spread the blanket on my black horse's back and reached for my saddle.

TWELVE

The letter didn't reach me until 5 May though the postmark said it had been mailed on 11 April. I include it here for any of you who might be interested in how this saddle tramp ended up.

Dear Ryan

I am sending this care of the postmaster, hoping you check your mail every once in a while. Spring has finally arrived and the wildflowers are strewn in profusion and the cottonwoods are budding out prettily. I am hesitant to write this as you are probably hesitant to read it. I have made my decision – if you still want me to travel out there, I intend to. A wagon train heading west has paused in Billings for supplies and to rest their stock. I have already made arrangements to travel with them. It's just as well, I am not a very good hairdresser!

Bobby will not be coming with me. He has made up his mind he wants to be a drover with a cattle ranch. I know it's hard work and dangerous, but as he has pointed out there are many cowboys his age or even younger doing such work. And it seemed so important to him to go out on his own and prove he was a man. I cried a little when he left, but not much. I had begun thinking about you all the time. You and me, that is. If you have not changed your mind, Ryan, watch for me when summer comes.

Bandon, Oregon! Isn't that a funny name? I hope it is every bit as beautiful as you say. Even if it isn't, I want to be there with you. Together we can build our lives into something very special. I know this. I do not know how long this journey of mine might take, but do not worry, Ryan. I may not be there while summer lingers, but I will be with you before the first snows fall.

Nina